The Color of Your Skin Ain't the Color of Your Heart

Books by Michael Phillips

Destiny Junction
Kings Crossroads
Make Me Like Jesus
God, A Good Father
Jesus, An Obedient Son
Best Friends for Life (with Judy Phillips)
George MacDonald, Scotland's Beloved Storyteller
A Rift in Time
Hidden in Time

CALEDONIA
Legend of the Celtic Stone

THE SECRET OF THE ROSE
The Eleventh Hour
A Rose Remembered
Escape to Freedom
Dawn of Liberty

THE SECRETS OF HEATHERSLEIGH HALL
Wild Grows the Heather in Devon
Wayward Winds
Heathersleigh Homecoming
A New Dawn Over Devon

SHENANDOAH SISTERS
Angels Watching Over Me
A Day to Pick Your Own Cotton
The Color of Your Skin Ain't the Color of Your Heart
Together Is All We Need

04B

The Color of Your Skin Ain't the Color of Your Heart

Michael Phillips

Bethany House Publishers
Minneapolis, Minnesota

The Color of Your Skin Ain't the Color of Your Heart

Cover photo of girls by David Bailey
Cover photo of plantation by Paul Taylor, index stock
Cover design by Kirk DouPounce, UDG DesignWorks

Published by Bethany House Publishers
11400 Hampshire Avenue South
Bloomington, Minnesota 55438
www.bethanyhouse.com

Bethany House Publishers is a division of
Baker Publishing Group, Grand Rapids, Michigan.

ISBN 0-7642-2707-6 (Hardcover)
ISBN 0-7642-2702-5 (Trade Paper)

Printed in the United States of America

Library of Congress Cataloging-in-Publication Data

Phillips, Michael R., 1946–
The color of your skin ain't the color of your heart / by Michael Phillips.
p. cm. — (Shenandoah sisters)
ISBN 0-7642-2707-6 (hardback : alk. paper) — ISBN 0-7642-2702-5 (pbk.) 1. Female friendship—Fiction. 2. Plantation life—Fiction. 3. Race relations—Fiction. 4. Reconstruction—Fiction. 5. Teenage girls—Fiction. 6. Orphans—Fiction. 7. North Carolina—Fiction. I. Title. II. Series: Phillips, Michael R., 1946– , Shenandoah sisters.
PS3566.H492 C65 2004
813'.54—dc22

2003021803

MICHAEL PHILLIPS is one of the premier fiction authors publishing in the CBA marketplace. He has authored more than fifty books, with total sales exceeding six million copies. He is also well known as the editor of the popular George MacDonald Classics series. Michael and his wife, Judy, have three grown sons and make their home in Eureka, California.

Contents

What We're Doing Here
1

As much as anything, I reckon you might say I'm a storyteller. And if you're new to my storytelling, which I reckon a few of you might be, I'll get started by saying that this is a story about two girls in the South in the year 1865. Of course, it's different than most stories because it's true. I'm just telling what happened. What happened to us.

What we'd been doing before you joined us is the same thing colored folks had been doing as slaves for years on the plantations of the South—picking cotton. I wasn't a slave no more, thanks to Mr. Lincoln, but we'd still been picking cotton as a way to make money and survive that year after the war between the North and South got done.

We'd been picking for weeks and we were still picking. On this particular day when my story gets started, when Katie and I, along with the others, went out to the fields to start picking cotton again, we had no idea that that same evening a set of suspicious eyes would be watching us from the woods. Neither did we have any idea that at that very moment someone was riding toward Rosewood who would change everything in ways that Katie and me couldn't have imagined in a million years. More for me even than for her.

But let me back up just a minute first.

After Katie paid off the first of her mother's loans at the bank in Greens Crossing, we came back to Rosewood about as happy as we'd been in a long time.

We were so tired! We'd been picking cotton from sunup to sundown for three weeks.

So when we got back late that afternoon, the four of us girls who were living together and who this story's about took baths. Then after supper we sang and danced and celebrated and went to sleep almost too tired to climb the stairs, but contented as we could be.

Katie—that's Miss Kathleen Clairborne, who you might say is the owner of the plantation called Rosewood where we live, even though she's only fifteen years old—she wanted to get right back out to work in the field the next day. We didn't *really* know who the owner was, but in the meantime, because we were the only ones there and she'd grown up there, she was acting like about as good an owner of a plantation as anyone could. That's how we'd got the money for the bank, by picking the cotton that her mama and Rosewood's slaves had planted earlier that spring before the war was over. And now from only having a few dollars left, Katie had more than a hundred fifty dollars in the bank. But I told her I thought she needed at least one day of rest. The cotton would still be there waiting for us the next day, I said.

By the way, my name is Mayme—that's short for Mary Ann. Mayme Jukes, that's what they call me. I'd been living with Katie for five months, ever since both of our families had been killed at the end of the war.

We had two other girls with us. Emma was a tall, scrawny, scatterbrained colored girl like me. She was real good-looking, though, which *wasn't* like me—so good-looking, in fact, that she'd got herself pregnant from a nearby white plantation owner who was now looking for her and trying to kill her and her little baby, who was called William.

So besides keeping ourselves alive after our families were killed, Katie and me were trying to protect Emma and William from anything bad happening to them. Another little girl called Aleta Butler was living with us too, whose mother had also been killed. She wasn't an orphan like us. Her father was still around somewhere and we didn't quite know what to do about him. But for now we were all four together trying to keep Katie's plantation going as best we could, without anybody finding out we were alone so they'd take us away.

I'd come to live at Katie's more or less by accident in April of that same year. Ever since then, the two of us had lived at her plantation house alone, milking the cows and making bread and butter, and taking care of ourselves. Katie showed me books and helped me learn to read better. And I taught her how to do things like milk cows and chop wood and sing slave songs. She read me stories from books and I told her stories I'd heard and made up. And it didn't take long before Katie was doing all kinds of things for herself. Even though I was older, and Katie was always telling me that she wouldn't have Rosewood anymore if it weren't for me, if anybody could have been said to be in charge around the place, it was Katie.

I was now sixteen, Katie was fifteen, and Aleta was nine.

I wasn't sure about Emma. I figured she might be a year older than me, but she could be so dim-witted sometimes it was hard to tell. But I'd learned to love her in spite of how she was. We'd both risked our lives for each other, and that can't help but draw people close together.

When Katie's mama's loan came due, at first we didn't know what we'd do. But then I was out in the fields and noticed how much cotton Rosewood had growing. I told Katie about it. Since the cotton was now ripe, we decided to see how much of it we could pick. It turned out to be worth more than we figured, and Katie got enough to pay off the whole first loan, even with a hundred seventy-eight dollars left over. At the same time, Katie had opened a bank account for me too—in my very own name—and put twenty dollars in it for me.

After taking the cotton into town, like I said, I told Katie we ought to take the next day catching up with our regular chores about the place and getting a little rest. Then the next day after that we went back out into the fields and started again on the cotton. Since we'd seen how much four girls could accomplish if they just put their minds to it and worked steady, it didn't seem quite so hard now, especially since for the last couple days before the loan was due we'd had help from one other person. He was a tall, soft-spoken black boy by the name of Jeremiah. I didn't know exactly how old he was either, but he seemed about my age, probably sixteen or seventeen.

I reckon I ought to tell you about him too.

Katie had known Jeremiah's father for a while. His name was Henry and he worked at the livery stable in Greens Crossing. He and Jeremiah had been separated for a long time, like slaves everywhere from the same family often were. But after the slaves had been set free, Jeremiah had searched for his daddy and had recently found him here and was now staying with him. Jeremiah found out what we were up to at Rosewood—pretending to operate the plantation without any grown-ups around. So far he hadn't said anything to his father or anyone else. So I guess you could say he was in on our scheme too, though we hadn't planned it that way. He was a strong and mighty fine-looking boy. At least in my eyes he was. I don't know if good-looking means the same in white people's eyes. My skin was a lot lighter than Jeremiah's, but we probably looked similar to white folks. I've sometimes wondered if all black folks look ugly to white folks. That's the idea you get when some white people look at you. Not people like Katie, of course. But I reckon this is just my way of saying that there were times as we picked at Katie's cotton that I found myself glancing at Jeremiah just because he was so handsome in *my* eyes, whatever anyone else might have thought.

As Katie and me and Emma and Aleta and Jeremiah were out again in the fields picking cotton, though not quite so fast and frantic as before, laughing and talking and I guess you'd almost say enjoying it—if a black person in the South could ever be said to enjoy picking cotton—we looked up and suddenly saw a rider approaching.

We'd had all kinds of loony schemes that we did when people came to the plantation to make believe Katie's mama was still here and make Rosewood seem normal. But now we were out in the fields and didn't have time to do anything like run and set a fire going in one of the cabins or hide Emma and William.

The rider caught us by surprise and there we all were for him to see. We stopped our work and stood stock-still, watching him come from the direction of the house.

Katie and I glanced at each other. Emma got a look of terror on her face, dropped her satchel, and ran to grab William from the buckboard where he was sleeping, then bolted for the house. I could see from Jeremiah's eyes that he was giving mighty serious consideration to bolting in the opposite direction. But then we all realized that to do something foolish like that would look more suspicious than anything. So we let Emma go and just stood and waited.

We didn't know it at the time, but Jeremiah's papa, Henry, was watching us from the woods while all this was going on. He'd been getting mighty suspicious about me and Katie for quite a while—suspicious, I reckon you'd say, in a good way, wanting to help us more than anything. But we'd still avoided him and tried to keep him from finding out about our scheme at the plantation.

As soon as his son Jeremiah got involved and knew our secret, however, that set Henry's curious mind going all the more. That's when he determined to find out once and for all what was going on. On that day he'd come out after his work at the livery and was now watching us all picking cotton and muttering to himself that he needed to have a talk with both us and Jeremiah and get to the bottom of the mystery of Rosewood.

But before he could think about it further, up rode the rider we had seen, and Henry sunk down out of sight where he'd been crouching at the edge of the woods. He watched for a minute or two more, then crept back deeper into the trees and went back to town without anyone seeing him.

The Stranger Who Wasn't a Stranger
2

As the rider came closer, suddenly I saw Katie's face change.

She gave almost a silent little gasp of astonishment, then her expression changed from fear to relief. And it wasn't hard to see why. She recognized him.

She set down her satchel and began walking toward him as he reined in.

"Well, now," I heard the stranger say, and even from where I stood I could see his teeth glisten white as he flashed a mischievous grin, "are my eyes deceiving me? Is this my sister Rosalind out in the fields again just like the last time I was here, or would this be . . ."

He hesitated, still with the grin on his lips, but also with a sudden faint expression of uncertainty, as if his own attempt at a joke had made him unsure for an instant who this tanned, sweating, hardworking girl actually was.

"It's me, Uncle Templeton," said Katie, walking up to where he sat on his horse, "—it's me . . . Katie."

"Well . . . Kathleen! You have turned into a woman since I saw you!"

He began to dismount. "And you look so much like your mama," he went on. "You've got her hair, her eyes, and—"

Before he could say anything further, suddenly Katie's uncle found himself smothered in his niece's embrace. Taken by surprise, he stood a moment with Katie's arms around him like he didn't know what to think. Then slowly he stretched his arms around her small shoulders and drew her to him.

"My, my," he said, "this is certainly an affectionate greeting for an uncle. If I remember correctly, you were a mite afraid of me last time I was here."

Still Katie stood, saying nothing, just holding him tight. The man was obviously uncomfortable. He relaxed his own arms and tried to ease away.

"Where's your mama, Kathleen?" he said. "I need to have a talk with her."

"Oh, Uncle Templeton!" said Katie in the saddest voice I'd heard from her in a long time.

"What's this I see?" he said, stepping back with his hands on both of her shoulders, bending down and gazing into her eyes. "Are these tears I see? My goodness, I didn't imagine seeing your long-lost uncle Templeton would cause such emotion. Come on, Kathleen," he added, "let's you and me go back to the house and find that mama of yours and have a nice visit."

He took Katie's hand and gave it a tug, then let go as

they started walking toward the house. "If I know Rosalind," he said, "she's probably working too hard like always, as I see you are too. And where's that daddy of yours? I expected to see him out here with a crew of workers. Instead it's just you and a handful of kids."

"But wait," said Katie as they slowly walked away, "don't you want to meet the others?"

"Who . . . them?" said the man, turning momentarily and glancing at the rest of us.

As his eyes came to rest on me for the slightest instant, a tingle swept through me and gave me goose bumps up and down my arms and on the back of my neck. I couldn't imagine why. I couldn't tell if it was fear or something else. There was nothing in the expression of his face that looked fearsome. It was actually a friendly, though kind of roguish face. There wasn't a hint of the hatred I'd come to expect from white faces after the war when they looked at "free niggers," as they called us. It was a nice face, and in his smile I saw a resemblance to Katie. It was obvious from one look that they were kin. And in a situation like we were in, kin meant something deep that nothing could take away, which was likely why Katie'd become so suddenly filled with emotion at the sight of her uncle.

But what made me tingle when he looked at me? I reckon it was from knowing that all at once our scheme was about to be discovered by a grown-up. It didn't seem there'd be any way for Katie to pretend to him forever. He'd come to see her ma and wasn't likely to be put off forever with being told she was away. And once he knew the whole truth, everything was bound to change.

What would happen to me, I didn't know. And what

about Emma and Aleta? But what would happen to Katie and Rosewood seemed clear enough. Katie and I had talked several times about her uncles and what would happen when they found out her family was dead.

Suddenly in the midst of our excitement, that day had come.

"Who's the little kid?" said Katie's uncle as he turned back, grabbed his horse's reins, and they continued on toward the house.

I didn't hear Katie's reply. I watched them go, my mind racing in a hundred directions. I didn't know what to do. Should I stay and keep working and pretend to be a hired former slave like we usually did when people came around? Or should I follow them to the house? If I did that, the man might think I was being presuming and start asking questions.

In the middle of my confused thoughts, I heard steps beside me.

"Who dat?" said Jeremiah softly.

I turned to face him. "Katie's uncle," I said.

"You know him?"

"I've never seen him before."

"Does he know?"

"No. But it seems likely he will before long."

"What you think he'll do?"

"I don't know."

Aleta now walked up. "What should I do, Mayme?" she asked. "Should I keep picking the cotton?"

I thought for a moment. "Yes . . . yes, I reckon we should, Aleta," I said. "You and me will stay here and keep working until we find out what's going on—or at least until

Miss Katie tells us what she wants us to do."

I turned to Jeremiah. "Maybe you oughta go," I said. "One less person for Katie to have to explain will make it easier for her." I tried to smile. "Thank you so much for your help."

"Don' mention it, Mayme," he said. "I jes' hope no trouble comes fer you."

"We'll try to get word to you. I don't know what Aleta and me and Emma will do if he makes us leave, but I'll come see you somehow, whatever happens."

Jeremiah nodded, then turned and began the walk back toward town, not knowing that his father was only a few minutes ahead of him.

Our Secret Is Out

3

KATIE WAS SILENT AS SHE AND HER UNCLE walked back toward the house.

Too quiet, her uncle was probably thinking. Like me, Katie's mind was racing in lots of directions, wondering what to do, and wondering if suddenly everything was going to change because we were about to get found out. He kept talking about her mother like she was going to come walking into sight any minute, and asking questions about Katie's daddy and brothers and why Katie was out picking cotton with a ragtag little group of kids and darkies. He hadn't seen Emma disappear into the plantation house itself, where she was now trembling for dear life as she hid with William. If he'd seen her, that would have stirred up even more questions.

Katie had hardly paused in her thoughts to notice how different her uncle looked than when she had last seen him when the war was still going on. It hadn't really been that long, only about a year and a half, but he had changed almost as much as Katie had. She told me once that he never came calling on his sister, Katie's ma, unless he wanted something, which riled Mrs. Clairborne a good bit. But Katie said that he always looked dapper as he could be, with ruffled shirts and jewelry on his wrists and wearing expensive coats and hats and boots.

And I reckon he was dressed that way now too. Yet his nice clothes were a little dirty and frayed. His black hair wasn't too well combed, and if I wasn't mistaken, both he and his horse had the appearance of having ridden hard and a long way. Both were dusty and tired and looked like they needed rest, water, and food. He didn't look like a man altogether at ease but almost like he'd been trying to get away from something.

They came past the barn and Katie's mind began to wake up a little. Just then she remembered the rest of us.

"Wait just a minute," she said to her uncle, then turned and ran partway back to the field.

"Mayme!" she called in a loud voice. "—Mayme . . . please come to the house."

"Who's that you're yelling at," asked her uncle, "—the little kid?"

"No, the colored girl who was out there with me."

"What do you want with her?" he said.

"She's my . . . well, I just want her, that's all.—Do you want to water and feed your horse?"

"Yes . . . that would be nice."

The minute I heard Katie call my name, I dropped my satchel and ran toward the house. Aleta didn't know what to do and slowly followed me a minute later. I didn't run all the way. I didn't want to seem too eager. Before I came into sight I slowed to the more lazy-looking gait that white men expected and tried to catch my breath. As I got closer, there was Katie watching for me with a frantic look on her face, glancing back and forth between the barn and the fields.

She ran toward me. "Mayme," she said in an urgent voice, "what am I going to do!"

"I don't know," I answered. "He's your uncle. What did he say?"

"He's just asking questions—mostly where everybody is."

We didn't have time to discuss it further. Her uncle came back out of the barn from feeding and watering his horse. He glanced toward us standing there together, and again that peculiar feeling came over me.

"Stay with me, Mayme," Katie whispered. "Whatever happens, I want you with me."

She walked toward him and I followed, keeping a step or two behind. They both kept going toward the house and I kept following, feeling mighty awkward and out of place, wondering what he was thinking about me.

They went inside. Katie's uncle took off his hat and pumped himself a big glass of water, then sat down on one of the chairs at the table almost like he owned the place, which for all we knew maybe he did now. I didn't stop to consider that he was Katie's *mama's* brother and wasn't kin to Katie's papa at all, which, now that I know how things work a little better, would make a big difference. All I knew was that he was kin and acted familiar and like Rosewood was his home.

Tired and worn though he looked, the man seemed like a dandy in my eyes. His white shirt had ruffles and bright buttons down the front. Showing from beneath the end of his fancy jacket were cufflinks sparkling from the ends of his shirt sleeves. I now knew what those were. If he wasn't rich, he sure dressed like a man who was.

I came and stood in the open door and waited. Katie just stood there too in front of her uncle, staring at the floor. He glanced around the place as he drank down the water and seemed to think it didn't look right. He looked over at me and this time held my face in his gaze a few seconds. A puzzled look seemed to flit through his eyes. But then he looked back at Katie, and gradually a serious expression came over his face.

"Kathleen," he said, "I think it's time you stop stalling. There's something you're not telling me. I know Rosalind's not on a trip—she wouldn't leave you alone or have left the place like this. Did she go into town? If so, she should have been back by now. I want to know what's going on here."

I was standing behind her, but I could see Katie starting to tremble.

"Kathleen . . . where's your mama?"

"Oh, Uncle Templeton," Katie suddenly cried, "—she's dead! They're all dead!"

She burst into the most mournful wail and began to sob, like a dam that had been held back all these months was bursting inside her. At the word *dead,* her uncle's face went ashen. Katie's wailing and sobbing left no doubt that she was telling the truth.

He sat there stunned, his eyes wide, his face white. Katie now walked toward him, put her arms around him, leaned her head down on his neck where he sat, and continued to sob. I heard Aleta come up the steps of the porch behind me. I turned to meet her and motioned for her to come with me instead of going in right now. I took her away from the house and explained as much as I knew about what was going on, which wasn't much. The last sound I heard as we crept softly down the steps was Katie's sobbing like I'd never heard her before.

We tried to busy ourselves with some clothes hanging on the line, but we weren't thinking about the wash right then. After a bit I told Aleta to go give the chickens some feed.

A few minutes later I heard the kitchen door open. Katie and her uncle came out. He still had the same stunned look on his face, and sure wasn't laughing or joking now. Katie and me had had a lot of death to get used to, and now I guess it was his turn. I couldn't help feeling almost more sorry for him than for Katie.

Katie had her hand in his and led him away from the house in the direction of where she and I had buried her family. Again I followed them, but from a distance.

Katie took him to the spot, then stopped. They just stood there looking down at the graves and the four stones we'd found to set by each one, not saying a word. Slowly her uncle stretched one of his arms around Katie's shoulders and pulled her to his side. She leaned her head against him and again began to cry.

How long they stood there like that I don't know. I figured they needed to be alone and didn't need my prying eyes staring at their backs. Katie had said she wanted me nearby, but she had her uncle to comfort her now. Whatever might happen later, at this moment that had to be a mighty important thing.

I turned away and went to see what Aleta was doing.

TEMPLETON DANIELS

4

FUNNY AS IT SEEMS TO SAY IT, MY MIND WAS BOTH relieved and full of anxieties and fears at the same time. As long and hard as we'd schemed to keep anyone from finding out we were alone . . . without warning it had happened. What we'd been worried about all this time had just suddenly happened.

Katie's kinfolk *knew*. Everything was bound to change now. Her uncle Templeton would no doubt take things in hand and do what grown-ups did. He'd put things in order and either stay here himself or find out who Rosewood was supposed to belong to if it wasn't him, and then maybe take Katie to live with him, though I had no notion where he lived.

Just when we thought we'd saved the day by paying off Katie's loan, it looked like our scheme was over, and our life together along with it. Without even consciously trying, my brain was working hard to brace itself for whatever changes this was going to mean, even if it meant that in a few days

I'd be gone from Rosewood and might not ever see Katie again. I found myself thinking again about that job at the hotel in Oakwood.

I fussed around outside the barn, not doing much of anything. After a while I saw Katie and her uncle walking slowly back from the graves and inside the house together. He still had his arm around her, and she was leaning against his side as she walked like it was the most natural thing in the world. And as nervous as I was about what all this might mean to us, it warmed my heart to see them together like that. Especially since I had no grown-up kin who would ever put their arm around me.

I've never been much good at doing nothing, so I went inside the barn and cleaned up a bit, then out to the stables to add water to the troughs for the horses and cows and pigs. When I had work to do, my worries were never quite as bad.

After a while I heard footsteps behind me. I turned to see Aleta.

"Katie sent me to find you," she said. "She asked if you'd come to the house."

I dropped what I was doing and followed her around the barn. When I entered the kitchen, Katie and her uncle were both seated at the table quietly talking. Katie's eyes were red. She glanced up at me and tried to smile.

"Hi, Mayme," she said. Her voice was still husky from crying.

"Hi," I said.

"I told him, Mayme," she said, sniffling and trying not to start crying again. "I told him everything . . . I couldn't help it. I hope you're not mad at me."

"Of course not, Katie," I said, glancing toward her uncle. "You had to . . . he's your kin."

As her uncle watched, he seemed moved by our obvious love for each other. But he was still looking funny at me. I was used to that. White folks always look different at blacks than they do their own kind. But something about the way Katie's uncle did it was peculiar. It made me feel funny in a way unlike any feeling I'd ever had.

"This is Mayme, Uncle Templeton . . . Mayme Jukes," said Katie. "She's the best friend I've ever had."

My eyes started blinking fast to hear Katie's words. It didn't seem like it'd do much good for both of us to start crying at a time like this. But it was all I could do to keep from it.

"I am happy to know you, Mayme Jukes," said Katie's uncle. "My name is Templeton Daniels, and from what Katie has told me, I suppose I owe you my thanks—for helping look after her, for helping look after the place . . . and for helping bury my sister and her family."

I nodded and forced a smile. I didn't know what to say.

"And I told him about Aleta and Emma too," Katie continued, "and—"

Suddenly Katie's eyes shot open.

"Oh, my goodness!" she exclaimed. "Emma! Where is Emma!"

In all the commotion we'd completely forgotten about her. All this time I'd figured she was upstairs trying to keep William quiet.

"Aleta," said Katie, "run upstairs and see if Emma's in her room."

Aleta dashed off and was back in less than a minute.

"She's nowhere up there, Katie," she said.

Katie and I looked at each other as we realized where Emma had gone to hide.

"Oh . . . poor Emma!" cried Katie.

She jumped up and we hurried into the parlor. The rug was thrown back and one look would have told us where she was, but neither of us had been all the way into the house since coming back from the field, and Aleta hadn't noticed.

I grabbed the door latch and pulled it open.

"Emma . . . Emma, are you down there!" called Katie into the cellar.

"Dat I is, Miz Katie," came a voice from below. "Me an' William's safe an' soun'."

"You can come up now.—We have got to fill one of those old lanterns down there with oil," she added to herself, "and put some matches down there too."

A second or two later, Emma's head appeared as she started up the ladder. She handed William up to Katie and then finished the climb and stepped out into the parlor. What Katie's uncle, who had followed from the kitchen, thought when he saw his niece holding a little half-colored baby, and the once-proud plantation house of his sister's family filled with two white girls and two black girls, it would be hard to say. And whatever those thoughts might have been, they could not have prepared him to see Katie give Emma a hug as her way of saying she was sorry she had had to stay down there so long.

Mr. Daniels just stood there for a few seconds taking in the sight, then slowly began to chuckle.

"Well, Kathleen," he said, "you may have told me, but I

must say this is quite a family you've got here! I've never seen anything like it in my life. It's just a whole family of kids! I can't believe you kept anyone from finding out all this time."

Emma, who had been busy taking William back from Katie, hadn't seen him standing in the kitchen doorway. At the sound of his voice, terror seized her and she started to bolt again, this time for the stairs.

"It's all right, Emma!" called Katie. "This is my uncle. I've told him all about you."

Emma paused and slowly came back toward the rest of us.

"This is Mr. Daniels, Emma," Katie added. "He won't do anything to hurt you."

"Right pleased ter make yer acquaintence, Mister Daniels," said Emma, trying to put on her politest tone for Katie's sake. "Is you gwine take care ob us now?"

Her words hung in the air for several long seconds. I saw Katie glance toward the floor. It was the unspoken question she and I had been wondering all this time. Suddenly Emma had just blurted it out. Katie's uncle seemed just as taken aback by the question as we were.

"I don't know, uh . . . Emma," he said after a moment. "Kathleen and I have a good many things to talk about."

"Well, she's 'bout the finest mistress in da whole worl', dat's all I got ter say," Emma went on. And once Emma's tongue got loosed, it was hard to stop it. "Miz Katie's been takin' care ob me, an' she an' Miz Mayme's been so good ter me an' my little William dat I don' know how I'd eben stayed alive wiffout dem. An' Aleta too, dey been takin' real good care ob her too, ain't dey, Aleta?"

Aleta nodded, still not sure what to make of all this.

Mr. Daniels laughed lightly, his countenance starting to get back its color and the humor that Katie said always went along with it.

"Well, Emma," he said, "I can see that Kathleen and, uh . . . Mayme here," he added, glancing toward me, "must have been working mighty hard and doing a lot of things right to keep the four of you alive—"

"Da five ob us, Mister Daniels. Don' forgit my William."

"Yes, of course, the five of you . . . to keep you alive and well all this time. I'm sure everything you say is true. She tells me that all the rest of you were a big help too. But as I say, Kathleen and I will have to talk it all over to see what's to be done now."

His words finally silenced Emma, and none of the rest of us had anything to say. What he'd said seemed to carry exactly the kind of overtones Katie and I had been worrying about.

At last Katie broke the silence by jumping straight into the middle of it.

"Does Rosewood belong to you now, Uncle Templeton?" she asked.

If Emma's question had hung heavy in the air, Katie's words sobered her uncle all the more. I reckon the poor man was having a lot thrown at him at once. He'd just found out that his sister was dead and that his niece had been running the plantation with an assortment of kids and blacks. And now suddenly his own potential future had changed as much as ours.

He glanced around the room and saw eight eyes staring

straight at him waiting for an answer. The prospect of Katie's question and all it entailed made him squirm a bit. Funny as it is to say it about a grown-up, I suddenly saw that he was maybe just as uncertain about what to do and what would happen as we were. When you're young you always figure that every grown-up is confident and never has doubts about things. But then when you start getting older yourself, you begin to realize that growing up doesn't take all the doubts about life away.

Mr. Daniels looked at us all staring at him, then chuckled a little nervously.

"I don't see how that could be, Kathleen," he said. "I'm no kin to your pa."

"Does it belong to Uncle Burchard, then?" Katie asked. "You won't tell him, will you, Uncle Templeton?"

"I've never met your father's brother. I only heard Rosalind mention him a time or two."

"I don't want to go live with him."

"We're not going to do anything until we have a chance to think this thing over a bit."

"If anything's going to happen, please stay yourself, Uncle Templeton," said Katie. "We'd all work real hard, wouldn't we?" she added, looking at the rest of us.

Nods and a flurry of *Yes'm, Miz Katie*s from Emma answered her question quickly enough.

Mr. Daniels laughed again at our obvious enthusiasm, though I could tell he was still squirming at the idea of it. Then he got serious.

"How old are you, Kathleen?" he asked.

"Fifteen, sir."

"Hmm . . . I see. Well, that's not going to help matters.

If you were eighteen it might be different. But fifteen . . ." His voice trailed off and I couldn't tell what he might be thinking.

"But Mayme's sixteen," said Katie hopefully.

Her uncle smiled. "I don't think that will do much good," he said, still reflecting on the matter. "No, that won't change things. It's blood relation that counts. And I'm afraid neither Mayme nor myself . . ."

Again his voice died away in a sigh. He turned and walked back into the kitchen.

The rest of us looked at each other with expressions of question and uncertainty. Slowly Katie followed him, then I followed her. We found her uncle sitting at the table in the kitchen just sitting there staring straight ahead at nothing in particular. He didn't even glance up as we walked in.

"Uncle Templeton," said Katie, "what should we do . . . now, I mean? What do you want us to do?"

Her words brought him out of his reverie.

He looked toward her, almost as if not understanding the question, or at least wondering why Katie would ask him what to do. It was clear enough that the notion of being responsible for other folks wasn't a feeling he was altogether acquainted with and was something that made him feel uncomfortable.

"I don't know," he said finally. "What you always do, I suppose—what you would do if I weren't here."

"It's getting kind of late," said Katie, glancing outside. "It will be dark soon. I guess we should fix some supper."

She looked at me. I nodded, thinking that sounded like a sensible idea.

"And we need to bring the cows in and milk them," I

added. "Aleta and I will do that if you and Emma can fix supper. I think I hear the cows bellowing already."

"After supper, Mayme and I will fix up Mama and Daddy's room for you, Uncle Templeton," added Katie, turning again toward her uncle.

But he hardly seemed to hear. He nodded and mumbled something about his horse, then got up and went outside. Gradually we all set about our chores. I didn't think about it at the time, but I reckon it was a mite strange that he didn't offer to help. In fact, he didn't come back inside till late. By then the rest of us had already finished eating.

Katie fed him and took him to the room, and I saw nothing more of him that evening.

Unsought Memories
5

By the following morning a few black storm clouds were wandering in. They seemed almost fitting in light of the cloud of uncertainty that now hung over Rosewood and our future.

I was almost timid to go downstairs, wondering what I might find. But I found nothing so out of the ordinary. Katie had gotten up before me and she and her uncle were seated in the kitchen. He was drinking a cup of coffee and laughing. They both seemed in good spirits.

"Good morning, Mayme," said Katie cheerfully.

"Kathleen has just been telling me," her uncle said, "about your suspicious store owner in town—what's her name?"

"Mrs. Hammond," said Katie.

"Ah yes . . . Mrs. Hammond. It sounds like she has been one of the chief obstacles in your scheme."

Whatever Mr. Daniels thought about me and Emma

sleeping in two of Rosewood's bedrooms, he didn't say anything about it or give any indication that he minded sharing a house with us. In fact, I would have to say that he didn't treat me any different at all. I couldn't remember a white person 'sides Katie using the same tone of voice to me as they did when talking to whites. But he sounded just the same when speaking to me as when he spoke to Katie. It was almost as if he didn't even notice that I was black.

"Uh . . . yes, sir," I said. "She's been a mite troublesome, that's sure enough."

"Well, she sounds like a woman I shall have to meet one day.—And I hear you and Kathleen chased away some men with guns who were snooping around here! You two have had some adventures, all right."

"He says the gold was Uncle Ward's, Mayme," Katie added to me as I sat down.

"And do you know if he's coming back for it, sir?" I asked.

"Naw . . . Ward's dead, as far as I know," he replied. "At least that's what I heard. I haven't seen him in years, and the last time I did there were men after him. I tried to pick up his trail several times, but it always went cold. Take the gold and use it, I say. He's never coming back."

"We already did," said Katie. "But it was only about fifty dollars. That wasn't enough to pay off Mama's loan."

"Hmm . . . I thought there was more. Those men sure think there is more," he added.

"Why, do you know them, Uncle Templeton?"

"I've run into them a time or two—that is, if it's the same bunch. They're convinced I was in on it with Ward."

"If there'd been more, we wouldn't have had to pick the

cotton," said Katie. "But we earned over three hundred dollars, didn't we, Mayme?"

Mr. Daniels whistled in astonishment. "That is a lot of money! It must have been hard work."

"It was. But it was worth it because we had a hundred and fifty left over."

"What did you do with it?"

"Most of it's in the bank, except for small money we kept to buy things."

They kept talking and I went outside for my necessaries and to get a fresh jug of milk from last night's milking. When I got back, Katie was still in the kitchen, but her uncle had gone back upstairs. Katie and I looked at each other with expressions of *Well . . . what happens next?* but didn't talk about anything much. We were a little quiet as we ate some bread and each drank a glass of milk, and as the day progressed just began to go about our regular chores and activities. Katie's uncle kept mostly to himself, tended to his horse, washed a couple of his shirts, and shaved and did man-things like that.

Later in the day I heard him and Katie talking in the parlor. I'd just come into the kitchen from outside and was getting myself a glass of water. I heard their voices in the other room. The mood between them was serious, not at all like it had been around the breakfast table.

I didn't want to intrude but couldn't help overhearing. Whether it was right or wrong of me I don't know, but I stood there and listened for a minute.

". . . just needed a place to get away for a while," her uncle had been saying as I came in, ". . . let the heat cool, so to speak."

Then I heard Katie's voice but couldn't make out what she'd said. A light laugh, but without any humor in it, followed. "To tell you the truth, Katie," her uncle said, "things have been a little rough for me lately."

"Rough . . . what do you mean, Uncle Templeton?"

"Just that a man like me doesn't always make friends, especially in my line of work."

"What kind of work do you do?"

Mr. Daniels sighed. "Let's just say that sometimes a man can try one too many schemes and it can come back to haunt him."

"I don't understand," said Katie.

"Well, maybe it's good you don't. But there is more than one place where I have worn out my welcome, shall we say. I told you, those men have been hounding me too and . . ."

His voice trailed off, or maybe he turned away. Then I heard him add, ". . . why I needed a place to come where I could hole up for a spell . . . but . . . didn't expect . . . more than I bargained for . . ."

He laughed again, though sadly this time. "I am sorry about your mama and papa, Kathleen," he said, ". . . a good sister to me . . . try to help you if I can."

We didn't pick any more cotton that day, or the next either, or the next day after that. With Katie's uncle there, everything was suddenly different. None of us knew what to do. He didn't say anything about what was going to happen, and Katie didn't want to ask. Sometimes he was boisterous and friendly, sometimes sober and thoughtful. He was more like a visitor than a family member. He didn't help and we did our chores and fixed meals and he ate with us and talked like everything was perfectly normal. The clouds kept coming and the sky kept darkening, which seemed to quiet us all the more. It was a strange couple of days. I was anxious to talk to Katie, and I knew the uncertainty was gnawing on her too. But I thought it best to wait until she brought it up. She had to work things out with her uncle first. She and I may have been friends, even best friends. But she and him were *family*.

On the afternoon of the third day since he'd come, I was upstairs in the room that we had been calling mine, which used to belong to one of Katie's brothers.

I sat down on my bed, or whoever's bed it was. All my old doubts had come back to plague me about my staying in a white man's home and sleeping in a white man's bed and taking the almighty presumptions I had. Everything Katie and I had done and been through together now seemed like a blur. I was again wondering if I should leave . . . or would *have* to leave. Katie's uncle was nice enough. I guess you'd say he treated Emma and me about as nice as any white man possibly could. I hadn't a single complaint. But he and Katie were *white,* and I was *colored,* and there wasn't any getting around that fact. I figured that one way or another Katie's uncle would wind up staying here with her and running the plantation now. I didn't see any other way it could be.

Unconsciously I found myself starting to go through the stuff in my room, looking at the few things I called my own, then at the things Katie had given me, looking at everything . . . clothes, her doll, mementos, my scraps of journal paper, and of course the nice journal Katie had given me and the pen and ink to write in it with and my mama's Bible.

I don't reckon I was consciously thinking of it, but I think I was again preparing to leave, like I had a time or two before, wondering to myself what things were really mine, and which I ought to take, and which I oughtn't to take.

I was quiet and a little sad, though I was happy for Katie. We'd been worrying all this time about her kinfolk finding out. But now that her uncle Templeton had, I saw that maybe our worries had been for nothing. He had turned out to be a fine man. It was obvious that he cared about Katie, and also that she loved him.

So it would all work out for the best, I tried to tell myself.

But still I couldn't help being a little downcast. And nervous. Because what was to become of Emma and me? She and I would probably have to leave and I'd need to take care of her. Even if Mr. Daniels might let *me* stay and work for them, he'd never let Emma stay. What white man would want to have her around? She was no earthly good for anything and just meant two extra mouths to feed. She had no one else. I couldn't very well let him send her away by herself. She'd never be able to survive, especially with William McSimmons looking for her. I'd *have* to take care of her.

Suddenly a sound disturbed me in the midst of my thoughts.

I turned around and there was Mr. Daniels standing in the doorway looking at me.

"I was just—" I started to say. But the sudden look that came over his face the moment I turned to look at him silenced me.

Obviously he'd known it was me when he stopped at the open door. But the instant his eyes met mine, his face went white and he almost gasped. It was such an expression that I couldn't take my eyes off him either. We just stared at each other for what must have been three or four seconds. Goose bumps flooded my arms and back and neck just like they had earlier.

Then his eyes wandered down to what I was cradling in my hands.

"Where'd you get that?" he said. His voice was so soft I could barely hear it.

"It was my mama's," I said.

If I didn't know better I'd have thought I almost saw tears struggling to rise in his eyes. He turned away, like he didn't want me to see him, and stumbled away and down the stairs. Half a minute later I heard the kitchen door open. I went to the window and looked outside. He was walking out toward the fields and just kept walking.

The next morning when we got up, Templeton Daniels was gone.

A Visitor From Town

6

I came downstairs thinking to myself that the house sounded a little uncommonly quiet. I found Katie sitting alone in the kitchen.

She glanced up at me with a different expression than anything I'd seen before. She looked older. It was both a relieved expression and a sad one, mixed in with almost a little bit of the feeling that she'd almost expected it, though hadn't realized it till after it happened.

"He left, Mayme," she said in a quiet voice.

She tried to smile at me, but then tears flooded her eyes and she looked away.

I walked over and put my hand on her shoulder. She leaned her head against my side and just cried softly for a minute or two.

"I don't know why I'm crying, Mayme," she said. "I ought to be happy. Nothing's going to happen to us. Nobody will have to leave. Nobody will find out. But . . ."

Again she sniffled and cried for a few seconds.

". . . but he's the only family I have," she went on, "or at least the only family who knows and who cares about me. And I had hoped . . ."

"I know," I said. "I hoped something good would come of it for you too."

It was silent awhile. Katie took a few breaths to steady herself, then glanced back up at me from her chair and smiled.

"So I guess life gets back to normal now," she said.

She stood, turned toward me, and embraced me. We stood in each other's arms for several seconds.

"You'll never leave me, will you, Mayme?"

"No, Katie," I said. "I'll never leave you."

She drew in another deep breath and stepped back, wiped her eyes, and smiled again.

"I'll be all right now," she said.

"Did he say anything?" I asked.

"No, just this," replied Katie, handing me a piece of paper. "It was on the table when I came down a while ago."

"What does it say? I can't read his writing."

Katie took the note again and read it aloud.

"Dear Kathleen," she said. "*There are some things I need to take care of. Right now things are a little complicated for me. I am sorry but having to care for you and the others is more than I can face. I am sorry about your mama. She was a good lady and I will miss her too. I know you and Mayme will be able to take care of yourselves until I figure out what's to be done. I'm sure you can take care of yourselves better than I could anyway. I'm sorry I haven't been a better uncle to you. Your secret is safe with me. Your uncle Templeton.*"

She stopped and brushed back a few remaining tears.

"I don't know why I'm so sad," she said. "But I can't help it."

"Do you think he'll be back?" I asked.

"I don't know," replied Katie. "With Uncle Templeton . . . you never know. And he . . ." she began to say, then paused and smiled sadly again, "and he took the money we had in the cigar box behind the sugar bin, just like Mama said he used to do. Why did he do that, Mayme?" she asked, looking at me with a bewildered expression. "If he'd asked, I'd have given it to him. But why did he just take it?"

I didn't have the chance to answer Katie's question. I didn't have an answer anyway. Just then we heard Aleta's steps coming down the stairs. Emma wasn't far behind her.

It took us a day or two, and then Katie and I started to think again about the cotton. It was ready to be picked and we couldn't wait forever, and her mama's second loan had to get paid. It was still cloudy and dark and a little chilly, but the next day we prepared to resume our work in the field. We didn't get out till the afternoon and only put in two or three hours at it. But that was enough to get back into our working routine.

The next morning, once we'd milked the cows and tended the other animals, all four of us went back out in the field to work again. It was tedious, but we were happy to put in a full day. We worked slower and went along in rows next to each other. Katie and me worked slow enough to stay even with Aleta and Emma in their rows. We'd been working two or three hours and the weariness had begun to set in.

"I think these rows are getting longer every time we

turn around," said Katie with a sigh.

"That's the way cotton is," I laughed. "It seems like it's never going to end!"

"I'm tired, Katie," said Aleta. "May we please stop?"

"Maybe it's time for a water break," nodded Katie, brushing her hair back from her face and standing up straight. "And we don't have to work as hard and fast now anyway."

No one argued with her. A water break sounded just fine!

We walked toward the wagon, where William was sleeping and where we had jugs of water and milk.

"Why we gotta keep pickin' dis cotton, Miz Katie," said Emma as we went, "when you already gib dat bank man his money?"

"I only gave him *some* of the money, Emma," replied Katie. "My mama owed the bank a lot of money and we still have another—"

Katie stopped abruptly.

I looked over at her. She was standing still as a statue. I turned around in the direction she was looking. There was a tall black man walking slowly toward us from between the long rows of cotton.

It was Henry!

Suddenly we forgot all about water! We just stood there stock-still as he walked toward us. I was sure that Jeremiah hadn't told him. But there was no way around his finding out now more than we'd wanted to tell him. It seemed like our secret was suddenly spilling out all over the place—was *everybody* going to find out?

He sauntered up and stopped and just looked us over

one at a time. We'd been trying so hard to keep what we were doing a secret from anyone in town, I figured we were in big trouble now. And I reckon I figured that the worst of it'd come on me. Black folks are mighty protecting of their whites, and when something's wrong they figure it must be a colored's fault. And the few times we'd seen Henry in town, the look he'd given me felt more than a little uncomfortable.

But Henry just stood there a few seconds. Then he finally spoke, and it wasn't what I had expected.

"Y'all got anudder satchel a feller cud use?" he said, like there wasn't anything unusual going on at all.

I took mine off and handed it to him. I wasn't quite sure what he wanted it for, but I figured I could use the big pockets in my dress for a while.

He slung it over his shoulder, then stooped down and started picking away on the next row beside mine. Katie looked over at me, and we all looked at one another, and then started slowly in again, none of us saying a word.

It was dead silent. All you could hear was our feet shuffling along the dry ground as we went back to where we'd left off and then slowly began inching our way from one plant to the next.

"Yep," Henry finally said, "eben wiff dose clouds up dere, a body cud git mighty tard in dese ole fields er cotton."

Again it was quiet, with just our feet moving slowly along the ground.

"Yep," he said again, "dis ole cotton'll make yo han's ruff an' red an' full er prickles. Ain't da kind er work mos' white folks eber done. Ain't dat right, Miz Kathleen? Right unushul work fer mos' white folks!"

"Yes, sir," mumbled Katie, keeping her head down.

Again we shuffled along in silence.

"You like pickin' dis yere cotton, Miz Kathleen?"

"Uh . . . I don't know," answered Katie.

"Who's dis yere frien' er yers, Miz Kathleen?" he said, looking toward Aleta.

"Her name's Aleta," said Katie.

"Well, Miz Aleta," said Henry, "my name's Henry. Wha'chu think 'bout pickin' dis yere cotton?"

"I'm helping Katie and Mayme," answered Aleta, her forehead crinkled in a scowl of uncertainty.

"Ah see . . . dat so?"

"Yes, sir?"

"Don' I reckernize you from ober Oakwood way?"

"I don't know, sir."

"An' what 'bout you?" he said, now looking toward Emma. "Who you be?"

Emma glanced toward Katie with big eyes of question. Katie nodded for her to speak up.

"Dat's right," said Henry. "You kin tell me. I'm jes' a colored like you what ain't gwine hurt you nohow."

"Emma," said Emma. "My name's Emma."

"*Emma* . . . I see. So dere's Miz Kathleen, Miz Mayme, Miz Emma, an' Miz Aleta all workin' out chere togeder, sometimes wiff a boy called Jeremiah helpin' 'em, ain't dat right. Mighty strange situashun it 'peers ter me."

There was a long silence. None of us knew what to say. Every now and then I'd try to sneak a look over at him. Then gradually I saw a grin come over his face.

He paused and looked up, shielding his hand from the

sun peeking out from the clouds.

"Gettin' kinder 'long tards da time mos' folks take er break from dere work," he said. "You ladies knows how ter fix a man somefin t' eat?"

"Uh . . . yes, sir," said Katie.

"Den I say we go t' yer house an' git somefin t' eat an' drink."

Without asking us any more questions, Henry straightened his back and stood up and started walking out of the field toward the wagon. Katie and I looked at each other, both of us silently saying, *What do we do now!*

Slowly we followed him. He dumped the cotton out of his satchel into the wagon, then walked off toward the house. Emma retrieved William from the buckboard and hung back behind the rest of us. Still not saying anything, we followed him and gradually he slowed down so we could catch up.

"An' a young'un too," he said as he saw Emma. "My, oh my . . . yes, sir, dis indeed be some kine er mighty unushul situashun."

I saw Henry glance over at the four graves as we approached the house. He sat down on the kitchen steps. Katie asked him if he would like a glass of water. Henry said he would. Katie went inside and pumped him out one and came back out to the porch and handed it to him and asked him if he'd like to come inside. He hesitated for a second, then stood up and followed the rest of us in, but just stood standing until she told him he could sit down. Finally he sat down at the table with the glass and took a long drink from it. The rest of us just kept standing there.

"Now, Miz Kathleen," he said, then looked over at me,

"an' Miz Mayme, ah seen dem stones markin' what looks ter me like graves out dere, an' ah got me an idea. But ah'd rather hear you tell me 'bout it yo'selfs."

He kept looking at us. Then slowly Katie started to cry. I walked over and put my arm around her.

Henry waited patiently.

"Yo mama and daddy's lyin' under dem stones, ain't dey, Miz Kathleen?" he said quietly after she calmed a little.

"Yes!" she whispered softly.

Henry got up from the chair and ambled toward us. He took Katie in his arms now and held her as I stepped back. Seeing how much he loved her made me realize he hadn't been trying to be mean with all his questions.

"It's gwine be all right, Miz Kathleen," said Henry. "Da Lord's watchin' ober you, an' He ain't 'bout ter ferget none er His chilluns—white, black, or any udder color."

Again Henry waited till Katie had calmed down. Then he looked over at me.

"What 'bout you, girl?" he said. "Yo mama an' daddy dead too?"

I nodded.

"Was dey Rosewood slaves?"

"No, sir . . . I lived at the McSimmons place."

"Ah see," he nodded. "Dat esplains why I seen you ober t' Oakwood dat day."

"Yes, sir."

"An' you, little girl," he said to Aleta, "yo mama an' daddy gone ter be wiff da Lord too?"

"Just my mama," said Aleta, taking a couple steps back, still not sure what to think. She'd got used to me by now, but a big black man like Henry was another thing. The look on her face said that she was intimidated by him, with a little of her old anger toward blacks coming back to the surface too.

"An' you?" he said to Emma.

"I don' know 'bout my mama and daddy," she said. "Dey wuz sold an' I wuz sold an' I don' eben hardly 'member dem. I ain't got no notion where dey is."

"Wha'chu doin' here?"

"I got myself in a heap er trouble an' I ran away an' Miz Katie an' Mayme, dey helped me."

"I see . . . well den, come here all er you," he said, opening one of his hands toward me and Aleta and Emma. "I reckon dese ole black arms is big enuff ter hol' all er you at once."

I went forward and he drew me toward him. I felt Katie's arm go around me too, and the two of us stood there for a few seconds in Henry's wide embrace. Emma followed and started blubbering like a baby.

Aleta hadn't moved but kept standing back. I think she was afraid of Henry.

Gradually we stepped away. Katie and Emma and I were wiping our faces and sniffing. It was such a relief having Henry hug us, not lecture us. He wasn't mad at all, like I'd expected him to be. I don't know why, but he was as compassionate as could be. Then Henry went back to the chair where he'd been sitting.

"What happened, Miz Kathleen?" he said.

"Some terrible men came, men on horses . . . they were shooting and killing."

"Where was you?"

"In the cellar."

Henry nodded. "I heard 'bout dem marauders, dey was called. How 'bout you, Miz Mayme?"

"The same men killed most all the slaves at the McSimmons place," I answered.

"When all dis happen?"

"Last April," said Katie.

Henry nodded again, then looked at Emma.

"Emma ran away from where she was," said Katie, answering his silent question. "There were people trying to kill her because of her baby. And Aleta's only been with us a couple of months. Her mama got thrown from a horse and hit her head. Aleta walked here to Rosewood and we didn't know where she belonged and so we tried to take care of her."

Henry nodded again and then it got real quiet for a minute or so. Henry was thinking and we were wondering what was going to come next.

"Are you going to tell on us, Henry?" said Katie. "Are you going to get us in trouble?"

"Well, I don' rightly know," he said. "Tell what? What is it dat you's so feared er folks findin' out dat y'all gotta sneak roun' town pretendin' an' carryin' on like y'all been doin'?"

"We're . . . we're trying to make people think my mama's still alive," said Katie.

"Why's dat?"

"So they won't put me in an orphanage and take Mayme away."

"What 'bout yo kin?" he asked. "As I recollect, yo papa's got a brudder somewheres?"

"Yes, sir," said Katie. "But I'm not sure exactly where

he is, and I don't like him. Mayme said if he found out, I might have to go live with him."

Henry glanced over at me.

"An' so Miz Mayme, she been tellin' you what you oughta do, dat it?" he asked, looking back to Katie.

Katie shook her head. "She tried to get me to tell somebody and maybe to go live with one of my uncles," she said. "But I told her I wouldn't. She was going to leave if I didn't, but I made her stay."

"An' what 'bout dat man who's been yere da las' few days? Looked ter me dat he was some kind er kin."

"You saw him?"

"I been watchin' an' waitin'. So's my boy. He ain't said nuthin' but I know he's been watchin' too."

"That was my other uncle," said Katie, "my mama's brother."

"I see . . . an' he knows too, does he?"

"I told him everything," answered Katie.

"An' what's he gwine do 'bout hit?"

"Nothing, I don't think. That's why he left."

"He ain't comin' back?"

"I don't think so."

"Hmm . . . seems a mite strange ter me, seein' he's kinfolk."

Henry glanced back and forth between us all again, seemed satisfied for the time being, and sat for a minute or two thinking.

"All right den," he said after he'd taken another drink of water. "I reckon da nex' thing's figurin' out what's ter be done 'bout all dis, 'cuz somefin's gotter be done, dat's fer sure, dat is, effen yer uncle ain't comin' back."

"Please don't tell anyone, Henry," said Katie.

"Who you think's gwine get you in trouble?"

"I don't know. Mayme thinks someone would try to take the plantation away if they found out my mama and daddy are dead, and make us all go away."

"Hmm . . . well, she may be right," he said, kind of mumbling and nodding his head, still thinking. "Yep . . . she may be right 'bout dat, though I cudn't say fer sure. But dis uncle er yers who was here, you ain't feared er dat from him?"

"Uncle Templeton's different. He's not like most white men. He liked Mayme," said Katie, glancing toward me. "And he was nice to us all, wasn't he, Mayme?"

"I reckon so," I nodded.

I finally got up and got us all some milk and cheese and bread and butter to eat. Nobody said too much. We were still anxious to know what Henry was thinking, and Henry just kept thinking and hardly saying a word.

After we had finished eating, he rose back up to his feet.

"Well, I got me some work I gotter tend to back at da livery," he said. "But I reckon I cud spare anudder couple hours er pickin' some mo cotton, dat is effen you's headin' back out dere."

He looked around the table at us.

"I guess we're going back out, shouldn't we, Mayme?" said Katie.

"I reckon," I said, standing up. "It's gotta be picked."

"An' why's it gotter be picked?" he asked.

"Because my mama owes Mr. Taylor at the bank a lot of money," said Katie.

"Ah yes . . . I sees now why you's been workin' at hit

so hard. Den we's gotter git it picked all right, an' soon. I'll sen' Jeremiah out ter help y'all termorrow, an' come out myse'f evenin's effen I can. Don' you worry, Miz Kathleen, we's git yer cotton picked."

He walked slowly toward the door and we followed him outside.

"What are you going to do, Henry?" Katie asked again as we walked. "Are you going to tell on us?"

"I don' rightly know yet, Miz Kathleen," he said. "Who wud I tell, an' what wud I tell 'em? But afore I do anyfing, ah needs ter spen' some time ruminatin' an' prayin' an' axin' da Lord what He thinks 'bout dis whole thing. 'Cuz it's da Lord who tells me what I'm ter do an' not ter do. So I got ter fix mysel' on what His min' is on hit—den I'll know what I'm ter do."

We watched him go, but didn't talk much amongst ourselves after he was gone either. Like she was with her uncle, I think in a way maybe Katie was relieved that Henry finally knew.

And Henry did pray too, just like he said. Back in town, he was thinking and praying long and hard about what he ought to do about us.

He went back to the livery stable and finished up his day's work. But he said he couldn't hardly sleep that night for thinking about us.

"Lawd, show me what I'm ter do 'bout dese chilluns er yers," he said he prayed over and over. "Dey's in some kine er pickle wiffout dere mamas an' papas, an' some kine er danger too, but maybe not so much as effen folks knew. An' since I'm da only one roun' 'bout dat does, I reckon I gots ter do what I can fer 'em, but you gots ter show me what dat is, Lawd."

The Storm
7

IF THERE'S ONE THING WE LEARNED TO DEPEND ON about Henry, he was true to his word.

As sure as he'd said it, the next morning we'd hardly finished breakfast and milking and getting the cows out when Jeremiah appeared walking into Rosewood from town.

He gave me a big smile when he saw me and my heart fluttered a bit.

"My daddy tol' me everything dat's goin' on here wiff you and Miz Katie," he said. "An' he said you's needin' mo help wiff da cotton."

Half an hour later we were out again in the field. It was so nice not having to pretend anymore. Katie was in especially exuberant spirits, and Jeremiah was more talkative than he'd ever been.

But the clouds hadn't gone away and it was chilly and windy. Dust was flying about, getting in our hair and eyes, and every now and then Jeremiah would look up into the sky and shake his head.

That evening Henry came out again. With him and Jeremiah working, the cotton mounted twice as fast. I don't know how they managed it, but the next day they both came out a little before lunchtime, and we finished the field where we had begun a month ago and got started on another even bigger one a little farther from the house. We had one wagon full of five hundred-pound bales sitting by the barn before we were done that evening, and another started. It had filled up in no time compared to before.

All the while as we worked that day it got chillier and chillier and windier, until finally Emma and William had to go back to the house. About an hour later Katie sent Aleta inside too. She was just too tired and cold and wasn't doing much good anyway and we didn't want her getting sick. Henry kept picking faster and faster and was mumbling to himself as he glanced up at the clouds swirling above us.

Gradually I began to feel the moisture in the air so thick you could smell it. We kept working almost frantically now, nobody saying a word. We were all thinking the same thing. I don't think Katie fully realized the danger, but she knew we couldn't keep picking in the rain and so she was working as hard, if not harder, though not so fast, as the rest of us.

Another hour went by. We were emptying our satchels into the wagon faster than ever and the loose cotton was piling up. But we didn't stop to stuff it into bales.

Suddenly the wind stopped. The air became calm and still and heavy and warm. We all felt the change and paused, glancing around.

Henry looked around in every direction, sniffing in the

air and still muttering. He looked worried.

"Hit's comin'," he finally said aloud. "Hit's comin' fo' sho'.—Jeremiah!" he called. "We gotter git dis yere wagon hitched up!"

Jeremiah looked at me and without another word we both started running for the house to fetch a horse.

Suddenly a terrific blast of thunder exploded above us.

"Hurry, Jeremiah—we ain't got no time ter lose.—Miz Kathleen," he called to Katie, "come wiff me . . . we gots ter git dat udder wagon under cover!"

Within seconds a few huge drops of rain began to fall on my face. Jeremiah and I reached the barn well ahead of Henry and Katie, who were hurrying as quickly as they could. Jeremiah glanced around. I grabbed his hand and led him to the corral. Three minutes later we were racing back to the field with horse and harness. At the same time Henry and Katie were just beginning to hitch up another horse to pull the full wagon of cotton we'd already baled into the barn and out of the rain.

As Jeremiah and I fussed with the harness, already my face was wet. Then another clap of thunder sounded and all at once the sky seemed to open. I jumped up onto the seat and grabbed the reins. Jeremiah leapt up beside me. I yelled at the horse and off we clattered toward the house as the rain poured down in torrents. By the time we flew into the wide-open doors, Jeremiah and I were soaked to the skin. My dress was clinging to me and water was dripping from my hair and ears and chin. The two horses were in a frenzy of excitement from the rain and sudden exertion and the close quarters of the barn. It was all we could do to calm them down and prevent them from hurting themselves, or one of us. Henry hurried quickly to them and began talking to them and stroking their noses one at a time while Jeremiah and I unfastened the harnesses and got them free from the wagons.

Ten minutes later the two horses were back in their stalls munching on some oats. Katie had just run back from the house with a handful of towels and we all dried our hands and faces. She was exuberant and flushed with the excitement of it all, still not aware of the danger.

After wiping his hands, Henry was leaning over the rail of the wagon of loose cotton, running his hand through it, reaching down to the bottom and pulling out handful after handful to feel how wet it was. Gradually Katie began to realize how serious Henry's expression was.

"It's all right, isn't it, Henry?" she asked.

"I reckon we got it in time though we shuldn't a waited so long," he said thoughtfully. "Effen dere's one thing cotton don' like it's gettin' too wet an' gettin' full er mildew. But dis is loose an' it'll dry up. An' fer dese bales," he said, now walking over to the other wagon and running his hand over the edge of one of the bales, "hit's tight enuff to a kep' much rain gittin' to it. I reckon Mr. Watson'll take it—he's a good man."

He sighed and glanced around, then walked to the big open doors and took a couple steps outside, where he stood under the overhang of the roof and stared out. The rain was pouring down in sheets so hard you could barely see the house a hundred and fifty feet away.

"Unforturnat'ly, Miz Kathleen," he said as he stood staring out into the storm, "hit ain't dis yere cotton I'm a worryin' 'bout."

"What do you mean, Henry?" asked Katie, walking up beside him and glancing up into his face.

"I mean hit's da cotton still out dere in dem fields dat we gotter be worried 'bout."

"Why . . . can't we just pick the rest of it when the rain stops?"

"Effen da rain stop soon, I reckon we might at dat," said Henry. "But it's gotter stop real soon, Miz Kathleen—*real* soon. Effen it rain like dis fer jes' anudder hour er two an' dat cotton goes down, den it's no good an' da whole crop be los'."

"Lost!" gasped Katie.

"Effen it gits soakin' wet an' full er mud an' hit's jest layin' dere in da dirt, ain't dat cotton no good ter nobody. Hit can't be picked den, Miz Kathleen—not when hit's down."

"But . . . but what about all the other plantations around? What about everyone else?"

"Dey mostly had dere cotton in an' under cover or sol' ter Mr. Watson weeks ago. Dat's why I been wonderin' what's goin' on at Rosewood when I seein' you bring in dem scrawny little bales so slow an' I'm wonderin' ter myse'f, *What dat Mistress Clairborne wastin' so much time fer—don' she know dat she's gotter beat da rain?* Dat's why I come out. But hit 'peers I was jes' a mite late 'cuz here's da rain an' dat cotton's still on da stalk."

The four of us stood there silently staring out as the water poured down. Beside me, I felt Jeremiah's fingers, then slowly he closed his big hand around mine. A tingle went through me. It made me feel warm inside, even though I was soaking wet. On the other side of me I glanced toward Katie.

Tears were falling from her eyes. I think she realized the rain wasn't going to stop.

FLOOD
8

THE RAIN DIDN'T STOP. IT DIDN'T LET UP FOR three days. I'd never seen it rain so hard. And when it finally did let up, it didn't stop but only slowed down a little. Already the streams and rivers had filled so full that a few of them were lapping at the top of their banks. As for the cotton, it wasn't just wet—half the field sat under two or three inches of water. The first big rainstorm of the year turned out to be the worst storm Shenandoah County had seen in a dozen years. That's what Henry told us later that folks were saying.

Katie was somber and so were the rest of us. From being so hopeful such a short time earlier, now our hopes of raising the money to pay off Rosewood's second loan were gone.

We didn't see Henry or Jeremiah again for several days. We didn't know it, but after the third day of rain we were cut off from them anyway. The river had come up over the road in several places and we couldn't have gotten to Greens

Crossing if we'd wanted to, or anyone from there to us.

We stayed inside, not doing much but trying to keep a good fire going and keep dry and warm. The cows, of course, couldn't go out to pasture and had to stay in, and that took more work because we had to feed them and clean up after them. None of us realized the danger we were in from the stream that wound west of the house. I'd gone down the road to keep an eye on the river, which was about a half mile northeast and then wound in closer by one of the cotton fields. And while the river was getting mighty huge and was spilling over the road in spots, it was still too far away from us to cause us any worry. But it's a funny thing about floods, sometimes the littlest streams can grow as big as rivers. And without us even realizing it, the stream that went through the woods at Katie's secret place was quickly becoming a river and was overflowing its banks. Though it wasn't moving fast, it was spreading out everywhere and flowing over the fields toward Rosewood.

Katie was the first to see it. She was upstairs one day and absently glanced out the window of Emma's room, a window facing west. All of a sudden she gasped in astonishment.

"Mayme!" she cried. "Mayme, come up here . . . there's a lake out there! A whole lake I can't even see the end of. The road toward Mr. Thurston's . . . it's gone. It's covered by water!"

By then we had all heard her and were running upstairs to see the sight.

I don't know if we were really in any danger. The house and barn and other Rosewood buildings sat on slightly higher ground than any of the surrounding fields. But seeing the water so close, and stretching out in three directions farther than we could see, was about as fearsome a sight as I'd ever seen in my life. The look on Katie's face wasn't just concern, it was a look of terror.

I don't think we had felt so helpless since we'd been together as we did at that moment. All four of us just stood there in silence. The sight struck awe into us. The raw power and terror of nature seemed so overwhelming, and we suddenly seemed so small and insignificant and powerless. And still the rain kept falling like it was never going to stop. I know we were all thinking the same thing—how much higher would the massive lake get . . . and how much closer to the house would it come?

It was Aleta who finally broke the silence.

"Is it going to come and swallow the house?" she said in a trembly voice. "What will we do, Katie?"

Her obvious fear brought Katie back to herself. Like she always did, she put her own fear aside to reassure Emma and Aleta.

"I don't know, Aleta," she answered, placing a gentle arm around Aleta's shoulders. "But if it comes to the house, we'll just stay upstairs. It could never get *this* high. It would have to cover all of Greens Crossing to do that!"

We didn't know it, but that's just what people in town were worrying about. We weren't the only ones with problems from the flood. Everyone for miles was looking at the rising water just like we were, and some houses and plantations were in far more peril than Rosewood. The bottom floors of a few were already under water.

Later that day, when Emma and Aleta were taking naps, Katie and I were alone in the kitchen. We stood for a few minutes just looking out. It seemed like that's mostly what we did these days, stand staring out windows into the dreary mist and slanting rain, wondering when it was going to stop. We both had serious expressions on our faces and were thinking the same thing—that maybe we ought to take a closer look at what was going on to see just how serious the danger really might be. Without a word, we went to the workroom next to the kitchen, put on big raincoats and galoshes and hats, then walked outside. We stood a moment more on the porch, then Katie led the way down the steps and into the rain.

"I think we should look at the river," she said.

I nodded in agreement, and we trudged off across the muddy yard, past the barn and stables, and in the direction of the old slave cabins, which had been vacant since the war.

We didn't get much farther than that. Halfway across the field adjacent to the last little shack, a field that sloped down from the high ground of the house and most of Rosewood's buildings, we saw the edge of the river lapping gently against the mud and stalks of cotton we'd picked. In just the few days since I'd checked the road, the river had come over its banks. Once it was that high, all the flat surrounding fields began to fill with its overflow. Out in the water beyond us the stalks poked up like the stubble of a white man's beard. The actual banks of the river were more than two hundred yards away from us. This was the closest place where the river came to Rosewood. But those banks had disappeared along with the two hundred yards. The river on this side of the house was so wide toward town we couldn't see the other side of it. Just like on the other side, the water looked like it went forever. Now for the first time we really realized that we were completely surrounded and cut off from Henry, from the town, from the whole rest of the world.

Rosewood was an island surrounded with water everywhere. We were alone.

Slowly we continued across the field through the mud until we came to the water's edge, where we stopped.

Again we just stood and watched, mesmerized by the awesome sight. Right in front of our feet, the water was shallow and calm and muddy. But as it stretched out into the distance, it was easy to see the flow of the huge expanse out where the actual river used to be. And it was moving fast, swirling and frothing like a torrent.

It was brown and muddy. Logs and bushes and sticks and small trees floated down past us out in the water as we watched.

"What if the river and stream both keep getting higher?" said Katie. "Rosewood's right in the middle of it."

"I know," I said. "The stream must pour into the river over yonder. That's what must be making the river so high. And you're right, Rosewood's right in the middle."

Before we could think any more about our worries, suddenly we heard a mournful moo and saw a helpless cow rushing by out in the middle where the river was moving fast, struggling to keep its head above water.

"Oh, Mayme!" cried Katie. "Can't we do something!"

"I'm afraid there's nothing we can do for it now, Katie. Once a river like this takes something, it's not going to stop till it gets to the ocean."

We watched as the poor cow disappeared and then we just kept standing there. If anything, the rain began to pound all the harder on our heads.

"I'm scared, Mayme," said Katie after a minute.

"I know," I said. "Me too. But we'll be okay. I'm sure the water could never reach the house."

"But it's only fifty yards away from the slave cabins."

"I know. But the house is quite a bit higher. Look—" I said as we turned around behind us—"the road goes up from the colored town. It can't possibly get much higher."

As we turned back around to face the swirling river and looked down, we saw that our boots were in the water. Just in the time we had been standing there, the river had risen another inch.

Without saying anything more, we both stepped back and slowly began making our way back to the house. Despite my optimistic words, I was worried too. If the water was rising this fast, there was no telling what might happen.

Dover and Red

9

DAY AFTER DAY THE DREARY GRAY CONTINUED, and the rain kept falling from the sky. Everything was gray and brown. The two brown rivers and lake of water surrounding us met the endless gray of the rain and sky off in the distance in every direction you looked, broken only in a few places by trees.

And still the water from the lakes surrounding us from the river and Katie's stream kept rising and getting closer and closer to the house. Three days after Katie and I had gone to look at it, the water from the main river had not only reached the furthermost slave cabin, it had completely covered the porch and floor and was rising up the outside of the wall and making its way to the others. On the other side of the house, the lake from the stream that went through Katie's secret place in the woods was lapping at the grass and trees in front of the house only a couple hundred feet from the porch.

But as frightening as it was to watch the water getting nearer and nearer, the worst of it was that the water was now trickling into the barn from the low-lying pasture next to it. That field wasn't connected to the river itself but had become a little lake of its own just from the rain. The cows were all clustered at the open and covered end of the barn where they could get out of the weather. We had no choice but to let the pigs take care of themselves in the rain and mud, getting what shelter they could in the little pig shed, where they crowded in on top of each other at night. Trying to feed them was horrible and messy but we did what we could. I suppose they were fat enough that a few days without food wasn't going to hurt them anyway. And there was certainly plenty of water in all the troughs!

The main problem was the five horses. Their stables too were half covered from an overhanging roof of the barn and opened into the outside pasture, where they mostly stayed when it was nice. But even the covered area sat at the low side of the barn, and it was the first to get flooded by the water trickling in from the fields. Almost from the first of the flood we'd had no choice but to take them all the way into the barn. There wasn't much room with all the equipment and the two full wagons of cotton, but there was no other place for them to stay.

But as the storm continued, though the cows made a terrible racket too, we knew the horses were most miserable of all. You could tell they were getting fidgety and restless, and though I was no expert about horses, I knew that when they got nervous they also got dangerous. Dangerous to themselves and to everyone else. And now with water seeping into the barn and turning the hard-packed dirt floor into a mass of mud, there was hardly a dry place for the horses to stand, and sometimes their hooves were two or three inches deep in mud and water because they didn't have the sense to stand in the few dry places left.

It was Aleta who surprised us with how much she knew about horses by alerting us to the danger they were in.

She had bundled up in hat, raincoat, and galoshes to go out one morning and help me feed the animals. As we were feeding the horses in the barn, she spoke up.

"The horses' feet are wet," she said.

"I reckon everything's wet," I laughed, thinking nothing of it.

"It's not good for them to be wet," she said.

"Why not?" I asked.

"Their hooves can rot and get infected."

"How do you know?"

"My daddy shoes horses. He knows all about them and I listen to what he says when he's talking to people. He says there's nothing worse than a horse with foot rot."

"What happens?" I asked.

"I don't know," Aleta answered. "But I've heard him say that horses aren't like other animals, and that they need special care."

I knew that too. Whatever made horses so beautiful and majestic also made them delicate.

"What should we do?" I asked.

"I don't know, get them someplace where it's dry."

"But there is no place that's dry," I said.

"There's the front of the house. It's grassy there and isn't so muddy."

"But it's raining. They'd get soaking wet and would still

be standing in the wet. And the water's only a stone's throw from the house."

"They could go up on the big front porch."

"On the porch!" I said.

"It's dry and their feet wouldn't get wet."

It sounded like a crazy notion to me. But if she was right about their feet, then I reckoned it was something that was worth thinking about. Later that same day I told Katie what Aleta had said and we went out through the parlor onto the front porch that looked out through the trees across the expanse of brown water.

The porch was huge and went the whole width of the front of the house and even around both sides between the big white columns and walls of the house.

"I think we could do it, Mayme," said Katie. "There's plenty of room for them here. They'd have more dry space than they do in the barn."

"But how would we keep them here?" I asked.

"Where else would they go? Everywhere else is wet. They wouldn't go out in the rain or where the water is over there, would they? Wouldn't they just stay on the porch to keep dry?"

"I don't know. Sometimes animals have minds of their own. They can be ornery. I don't know . . . maybe it's worth a try."

"How would we get them up on the porch?" asked Katie. "What if they don't want to go up on the boards?"

"You put oats there," said Aleta, who had been following us and listening to every word we said. "I heard my papa say that a horse will always follow feed if it gets hungry enough."

Katie and I looked at each other.

"I reckon it's worth a try," I said.

So we set off to start making preparations. In an hour we had lugged a small feed trough around to the front of the house and put a bucket filled with water beside it. Then we dumped a bucketful of oats in the trough.

"Shall we bring the horses from the barn?" said Katie excitedly. I guess we were all excited just to have something to do after all the dreary days of endless rain.

"Probably not all at once," I said. "We better let them get used to it a little at a time. Horses can get mighty jumpy when they get nervous."

"Let's bring one or two, then," she said as we walked back around to the barn still wearing our rain clothes. "Red and Dover are older and calm most of the time."

"That's good," I said. "We'll start with them and when they get used to it, we'll bring the other three."

Five minutes later I had one of the big barn doors open and Katie was leading the two horses out with ropes around their necks. She was talking gently to them, but they seemed happy enough to go with her and get out of the barn, where they'd been cooped up so long.

They snorted and moved around as if the fresh air and rain and wind was filling them with energy. We walked around the house to the front, their hooves thudding and sloshing in the mud and wet grass.

We reached the steps leading up to the porch. There were only three steps.

The two horses hesitated as Katie walked up onto the porch. She gently tugged on the rope and then they came. But you could tell they didn't like the idea of the steps or the feel of the wood beneath their hooves. They clomped up all agitated and fidgety, then one of them looked like it was going to rear.

"Look out, Katie!" I yelled.

"Here, Mayme, take Red," she called back to me, tossing me the rope. "—Dover . . . Dover," she went on to the skittish horse, "it's all right . . . there are some oats over here."

But by then Dover was moving all about, his feet kicking and clattering and making a racket on the wood.

Luckily I'd managed to get Red's nose stuffed into the trough where we'd put the oats and I gently tied the rope around one of the porch columns and went to try to help Katie. Aleta, who had been following us, now began stroking Red's nose and talking to her.

But Dover was getting more and more agitated every second.

"I don't know why he's so nervous," said Katie. "I don't think this was such a good idea! We need to get him off the porch so he can calm down!"

I couldn't have agreed more. As content as Red seemed to be to eat oats out of the rain up on the porch, Dover was dangerously excited.

But just when it seemed things couldn't get worse—they did.

Emma had been upstairs trying to get William to sleep during all the commotion and didn't know what we were doing.

All of a sudden the front door of the house opened and out she walked, leaving the door wide open.

"What all dis racket?" she began, bumping straight into

a huge brown flank that had backed up a couple steps just at the moment she'd come through the door.

"Laws almighty . . . what dis fool horse—"

But she didn't have the chance to say anything else. And neither did the rest of us, for that matter.

Spooked all the more by Emma's sudden appearance on the other side of him from where Katie was trying to calm him down, Dover reared and whinnied and yanked the rope from Katie's hand. The next instant he bolted past Emma and through the open door, and disappeared into the house.

"Oh no!" cried Katie. "Mayme!"

We ran inside after him, Emma following us, babbling away with a flurry of questions.

Dover was clomping around the parlor in a frenzy of snorting and terrified whinnies and prancing hooves. He'd already emptied himself and made a big mess on the carpet and was in danger of breaking all the furniture and hurting himself really bad.

"Emma," I said, "please go back outside."

"But, Miz Mayme, what's—"

"Please, Emma . . . right now."

Fortunately for all of us, she was too scared to argue anymore and went back outside.

"We've got to calm him down!" I cried to Katie.

"How, Mayme!"

"Can you get the halter?"

"I'm trying . . . let's sit down, Mayme. Let's both sit down and maybe that will calm him some."

Anything was worth a try. We sat down and stopped talking. By then he'd already upset several upright chairs and I was afraid he might even knock over the gun cabinet. He continued to prance around the room but gradually began to settle down. We kept sitting, and finally he seemed to notice Katie and began snorting and slowly walking over to her. Katie reached out a hand. Dover snorted and sniffed at it as gradually Katie started stroking his nose. Still we just sat to let him calm down some more. Finally Katie stood, the rope now in her hand again, and led him back outside through the door, straight off the porch, and down onto the wet grass.

I followed just in time to see Dover break loose again, obviously preferring the wet and rain to the parlor, and bolt across the grass in a full gallop. He wasn't able to go far, however. Within a few seconds he had run out of grass and was splashing through the flood-lake amongst the trees.

Katie and I just stood watching, relieved to have him off the porch and out of the house. Then Aleta, who had been stroking Red's long nose the whole time, spoke up.

"Somebody's coming," she said.

HENRY
10

HENRY HAD BEEN WORRYING ABOUT US EVER since a couple days after he'd left us the day the rain had started. Hearing how bad the flood was and about several of the other plantations reported to be underwater, he'd gotten more and more concerned with every day that passed.

Where he'd gotten the small boat, and how he had managed to maneuver it across the huge expanse of water without getting swept into the river on the other side of the house, I couldn't imagine.

But there he was, rain pouring down on him, rowing toward us over the water!

"It's Henry!" cried Katie.

She ran from the porch and across the grass toward him. She kept going right into the water and walked as far as she could until the water was up to her knees and completely over the tops of her galoshes.

"Henry . . . Henry!" she called when she could go no farther.

When he was close enough he tossed her a rope and she pulled on it and began trudging back toward the house, tugging on it as she went.

Two or three minutes later, she and Henry were walking toward the rest of us across the grass. Katie was beaming, almost as if she'd rescued him from the flood.

"I figgered I oughta see how you ladies wuz gettin' on wiff all dis rain," he said. "I don' mind tellin' you dat me an' Jeremiah wuz a mite worried."

"So were we!" laughed Katie.

"But how did you get here?" I asked.

Henry began to chuckle. "Dat wuz a mite ob a challenge, all right," he said. "Let's jes' say I went da long way roun', up dere pas' da Thurston place, den floated down dis way an' made my way 'cross all dat water afore da river could git me.—So has dis flood done you no harm roun' Rosewood?"

"No, we're fine," said Katie. "Aren't we, Mayme?"

"I reckon so . . . all except for the horses," I added, laughing.

"I see one ob dem up dere on da porch, an' anudder runnin' 'bout yonder. What dey doin' dere?"

"We thought they might be safer out of the barn, where it was dry," said Katie, who then briefly told Henry what we'd tried to do.

"An' jes' what put a noshun like dat inter yo heads, Miz Kathleen?"

"Aleta told us that their hooves might get infected if they stood too long where it was wet, and the water's getting into the barn pretty bad. It's coming in from the pasture."

"I see—did she, now?" nodded Henry. "I'm a wonderin' how Miz Aleta figgered dat out."

"She said her father's a blacksmith and knows about horses."

"Did she, now?" nodded Henry, taking in the information thoughtfully.

All at once Katie realized what she'd done. We looked at each other, wondering what Henry would do. The look on his face said that he was turning the thing over in his mind. If Aleta's father knew horses, there wasn't much chance that Henry wouldn't know him if he lived anywhere for ten miles around.

Whatever Henry was thinking, he didn't pursue it right then.

"Well," he said after a bit, "I reckon Miz Aleta's right 'bout dat. But on da udder han', da danger ob hoof rot ain't so bad as da danger ob dem slippin' an' breakin' a leg on da slippery boards ob a porch, spechully when dey start makin' a mess beneath them. Dey's jes' a mite too skittish fer a place like dat effen you ax me."

"Dover already broke loose and got into the house," said Katie.

"I can't say I's surprised, nohow," said Henry. "Well, hit wuz a good idea, but why don't you show me jes' how bad it is in dat barn, an' den we'll see what's ter be done. Meantime, looks like Red here's content fer a spell longer, an' unless I's mistaken, ol' Dover's ready ter foller us back ter da barn."

We walked back around the house.

"Looks like dat rain's finally lettin' up," said Henry, gazing up at the sky.

I hadn't even noticed. But now that I did, I saw that he was right. The rain had changed to a drizzle.

"How long will the rain last, Henry?" asked Katie.

"Hard ter say, Miz Kathleen. Folks roun' 'bout is plenty worried, I kin tell you. From da looks ob it, you's doin' right well. But dere's some folk's houses whose kitchens already got water ober da floor."

An hour later we were all back in the house having something to eat and warming up and Henry drinking the coffee we'd made for him. The horses were safely back in the barn after our adventure of trying to move them. We could smell the evidence of Dover's brief flight into the house from the other room, which we'd have to clean up later.

We were laughing and in good spirits to have Henry there and not to feel so alone and isolated—though speaking for myself, I wished Jeremiah had come with him.

"Well, I's jes' glad ter see you ladies ain't no worse fer all dis flood, an' I reckon yer critters'll come through it jes' fine too."

"What will you do now, Henry?" asked Katie.

"I reckon I'll git back in dat dere boat an' try ter ride dat stream down across da river."

"That seems too dangerous!"

"I reckon it is a mite at dat," chuckled Henry. "But da water don't bother me none. When I wuz a boy I wuz a slave way west ob here on da Mississippi. Why, I cud tell you stories ob dat blame river dat'd make yo eyes pop right outta yer head."

"Oh, tell us, Henry!" said Katie excitedly. "I want to hear about it!"

Henry kept laughing to see Katie's enthusiasm.

"Well, maybe da time'll come fer dat one day," he said. "But you kin see dat no little river like dis is gwine worry me."

"You call dis a little river . . . even with da flood!" exclaimed Emma.

"You should see dat Mississippi in springtime," said Henry. "Hit always looks like dis, an' dat's when it ain't floodin'! No, chil', dis yere water don't put no fright inter me, nohow."

But it was already getting late in the day, and Katie convinced Henry not to start back for Greens Crossing but to stay the night at Rosewood.

That was another adjustment for us all to make. Just when we got used to one change, it seemed there was another one to face, just like Aleta having to get used to seeing Katie treating me like a friend, and then walking into the house and seeing *another* colored girl living under Katie's roof. It was a good while that we'd been getting on together like a family, all of us used to one another and the others' ways of doing things, all of us knowing it was Katie's house and that she was the one who was in charge. I guess we'd all had to get used to each others' peculiarities too. Maybe that's part of what being a family is.

So it was strange to see how we all reacted to having a grown-up around—and a colored one at that! Katie, of course, was the most color-blind of us all and was excited as could be. The minute Henry agreed to stay, she started talking about what to fix for supper and wanted to make him something special, like he was the president or something. But Aleta was a little subdued, because every once in a while Henry would eye her like he was still thinking about her more than he was letting on. Henry'd been around enough that all of us were used to him and knew he was our friend and wanted to help us. But having him there for the evening and all night . . . it just made it different—like we had to get used to him all over again.

And it's a funny thing about colored folk—as much as we talk about white folks treating us different, we treat each other different too. Black folks are mighty particular about how they expect other black folks to act, especially around white folks. They don't want any other colored person taking liberties or getting too familiar with *their* whites. And so as much as I'd come to love Henry, all of a sudden I found myself watching him out of the corner of my eye to see how he was with Katie, making sure he didn't take too many liberties or speak too familiarly with her, making sure he behaved himself under Katie's roof.

It was silly, of course. Look at all the liberties *I'd* taken! Katie'd let me carry on practically like Rosewood belonged to me . . . and yet now I was watching Henry to make sure he didn't get too uppity. No colored likes to see another colored acting uppity. I reckon it goes to show that even though I was black, I was still more bound to thinking about a person's skin color than Katie was. And I could tell Emma was looking different at Henry too. If he'd been white, we'd have known where we stood and would have known how to act. But him being colored changed everything.

But one thing we wouldn't have had to worry about in

a million years was Henry getting uppity. He didn't have an uppity bone in his body. He was completely respectful of Katie, and all the rest of us too. He treated me like I was white and always called me *Miz Mayme*.

When it was ready, we sat down to supper. As we were starting in, Henry looked around at us and said, "Ain't you fergettin' somefin?"

I didn't understand what he meant at first. But when he bowed his head and closed his eyes, I realized he was wondering why we hadn't asked God's blessing. It just hadn't been something that Katie and I'd got in the habit of doing, I reckon.

"Dear Lawd," Henry prayed, "we thank you fer yo provishun fer us, an' fer watchin ober us. Show us what ter do, an' protect dese dear ones er yers. Amen."

Aleta was still silent as stone around Henry. When I opened my eyes after he was done praying, she was sitting there staring at him. But if she'd got used to me, I reckon she'd get used to him eventually too.

The rain had started up hard again, but we were happy and warm inside. After supper Henry told us story after story about his boyhood on the Mississippi and had us laughing so hard, even Aleta. I hadn't realized how much I'd missed listening to the old colored uncles tell their stories. We didn't blow out the lanterns for bed until so late in the night it was probably the next morning.

As much as Katie protested, Henry wouldn't hear of sleeping in the house.

"You jes' gib me a blanket er two an' I'll be happy as can be in da barn wiff the horses. I'll fin' me a dry bed ob straw an' I'll sleep like a baby."

THE SUN AGAIN
11

WHETHER IT WAS HENRY'S COMING AND knowing somebody was watching out for us, or just not feeling so alone, as I lay in bed that night I felt more hopeful than I had in days. I drifted off to sleep, listening to the rain on the roof above me, feeling content and happy.

I woke up in the middle of the night. It was pitch dark, but something felt strange. I lay there in the silence wondering what it was. Then suddenly it dawned on me—it was the *silence*. It was absolutely quiet.

The rain had stopped!

Gradually I drifted back to sleep. When I next woke up I was in for a surprise. Sunlight was streaming through the windows! It was so bright and unexpected it almost blinded me when I opened my eyes.

"Katie! Katie!" I cried, jumping out of bed and running to Katie's room. "The sun's out. The rain's stopped!"

A few minutes later, all four of us were standing at one

of the upstairs windows looking out. There wasn't a cloud in the sky, which was so brilliant a blue I'd almost forgotten what it looked like. The sun made the brown water stretching out across the fields all the uglier. What was normally mostly green, wherever we looked, had been replaced by brown as far as you could see, until it met the blue of the sky at the horizon.

How could there be so much water? Was this how Noah had felt?

"Let's go look at the post!" said Aleta excitedly. "I want to see if the water's gone down."

"You'll have to get dressed first," laughed Katie.

We all scurried back to our rooms and then ran downstairs, got on our galoshes, and hurried outside. We had been watching the level of water on an old fence post in the field past the barn that had a lot of knots on it so we could see the water rising. We had to get boots on to get close enough. Gradually we inched through the water until it was nearly to the top of our boots. We stopped about ten feet from the post.

"The water's gone *up* since yesterday!" said Katie. "How can it go up when the rain's stopped?"

Just then we heard a deep chuckle behind us.

"Da flood don't care 'bout no rain," said a voice we knew instantly to be Henry's. We turned and saw him moving toward us in his bare feet with his trouser legs rolled up. "Effen dere's still water comin' down from upriver, hit'll keep risin', maybe even fer a day er two."

We turned and all began sloshing back toward the house.

"I still don't see how that can be, Henry," said Katie.

"Hit's jes' the way rain an' rivers an' floods is, Miz Kathleen."

"But is the flood over?"

" 'Peers likely, effen we git no mo rain fer a day er two, an' dat looks promisin' wiff dis sun shinin' out. Once da water gits as high as hit's gwine git an' starts back down, dis ol' flood'll be gone in no time."

"Will you wait till then to go back to town, Uncle Henry?" asked Aleta.

"No, chil'," laughed Henry. "I can't do dat. Effen you can gib me a good cup er coffee, I's be on my way. I gots ter git back ter work."

"We'll give you breakfast to go with your coffee," said Katie. "But how will you get back?"

"Same way's I come—rowin' out yonder 'cross dat water on da other side ob da house."

Two hours later, Henry got in the little rowboat and headed out across the flat brown sea.

"But what if the current takes you into the river?" said Katie, still worried about how Henry could possibly navigate what looked like an ocean.

"Don't you worry none 'bout me, Miz Kathleen. Effen I git too far down an' da river takes me, den I'll jes' point dis yere boat inter dat current an' ride as fast as hit wants ter go till I can work my way to the udder side. You neber fight a current—you go wiff it till you gets across it."

Even as he spoke, Henry was moving away from us with great pulls on the two oars, and pretty soon he was heading out into the middle of the water.

"I'll be seeing you ladies as soon as dis water's all gone!" he called back to us.

Aleta waved one last time. I looked at her face and saw that she was a little frightened as she watched Henry row out into the middle of the water.

"I don't want anything to happen to Uncle Henry," said Aleta.

"He'll be safe," I said.

We watched until he was out of sight, then went back into the house.

The sun kept up for two days. By then, like Henry had said, the water had started to recede. It rained a little more on the third day but not enough to do any harm, and then the sun came out for good.

Eventually the water began to subside even more quickly. But it took a week for the river and streams to fall back down to their former courses. And when they did they left a mess of everything.

All the remaining crops were gone. The fields didn't even look like fields anymore, just brown mud everywhere.

Within two weeks the river and stream were almost back to normal.

And gradually life got back to normal for us too, although I don't know what normal actually meant. Was anything about Katie's and my life *normal?* Or would it ever be?

As close as the water had come, Rosewood wasn't too much the worse for the flood, except for one of the old slave cabins, that is. When the water went down and the surrounding area started to dry up, and Katie and I went on our first walk about, we discovered that the cabin closest to the river wasn't even there. The flood had taken it, and it was just gone!

Other than that we saw no damage.

The barn dried out, then the pasture, and pretty soon we were able to let the horses and cows back outside. Even the cows frolicked a little at first, and the horses ran and ran from fence to fence the whole length of the pasture. It was some time, however, before we could take the cows out to any of their usual fields, since they were covered in mud. It took several weeks both for the mud to dry up and the grass to start growing back up through it again. But eventually the green returned to the fields and woods and landscape.

There was one place that didn't return to green—the enclosed area around the pig shed. It remained a muddy, stinky, brown mess all through the winter!

Looking Ahead

12

ONE AFTERNOON KATIE LEFT THE HOUSE AND said she wanted to go to her secret place in the woods to see how much damage the flood had caused to it.

I was curious myself, but I knew that if Katie had wanted me to go with her, she'd have said so. There are some things a person's got to do alone. Emotions and thoughts don't stir around inside you in quite the same way when other people are around, and the kinds of thoughts and feelings that get moving when you're alone are good for you. I knew this was one of those times for Katie. She'd been going to her place in the woods since she was a little girl. It was where she learned to get in touch with herself and nature, where she learned to write poems and think and pray. And now that she was slowly becoming a woman, it was important to touch some of those things of the past every once in a while to feel whatever they might make her feel and let those feelings mature her all the more. It's the same way it had been for me when I'd wanted to go back to the McSimmons place.

She returned about an hour later. She was in a quiet mood.

"It was sad, Mayme," she said. "All the green was gone and it was muddy everywhere. But at least the big rock hadn't gotten washed away. And everything will grow back."

She sighed and smiled. "I was thinking on the way back to the house," she went on after a minute, "that if the water could change the landscape so much, what if it got into the cellar during the flood. So I thought we should look."

We went into the parlor, pulled back the rug, and lifted the door in the floor.

"Oh, we'll need a lantern," said Katie as she began to step down into the darkness. "Would you mind getting one from the kitchen?"

A few minutes later we were standing down on the hard dirt of the cellar looking about. Nothing was changed. And except for a little wetness in two of the corners and along one of the walls, there was no sign of the flood.

Katie glanced about. There wasn't much there, just the old chest where we'd found her uncle's clothes and a few pieces of old furniture with stuff heaped on it, an oak barrel for storing potatoes, several lanterns that looked like they were rusting, and some shelves with a few things piled on them.

"It looks all right," said Katie. "At least the flood didn't ruin everything.—Maybe I should bring one of those lanterns up," she said, walking over toward where the furniture had been stored.

She tried to pick up the largest of them, an old ornate oil lantern of brass with a huge round base.

"Ugh!" she said. "It's too heavy!"

"Do you want some help?" I asked.

"No, we'll get it later if it turns out we need it." We climbed back up into the house and closed the door after us.

The flood had come on us so suddenly in the middle of our picking cotton that we hadn't really had the chance to think or talk about what it might all mean. But I came on Katie one day in her papa's office sitting at the big desk of her mama's going through papers again.

"What are you doing?" I asked.

She looked up and smiled kind of sadly.

"Just looking at all of this and seeing if I can make sense of it," she answered.

"Can you?"

"Not much. But with picking the cotton and everything, I'd been so excited about paying off that loan to Mr. Taylor that I hadn't really thought much about the second loan. With all the cotton I thought we were going to pick, especially with Henry's and Jeremiah's help, and with the money that's still in the bank, I wasn't even thinking about it or worried about it. But then the storm came and now there's not going to be any more money coming from anywhere."

"Don't you think what we got will be enough?" I asked.

"I don't know. The money left over from the first time wasn't enough. That's what Mr. Taylor said."

"What about the cotton piled on the wagons in the barn?" I asked.

"I don't know," said Katie. "But it's not as much as we picked the first time—before Henry and Jeremiah came. It's only two wagons and one of them isn't even full."

"When should we take those wagons into town?"

"I don't know. Maybe we should ask Henry."

Next time Henry came out to check on us after Shenandoah County was starting to dry out, we did ask him. He said he'd try to find out how prices were and whether we ought to sell it now or keep it through the winter.

"But what you worried 'bout money fo', Miz Kathleen?" he said.

Katie glanced at me. I knew she was wondering how much to tell him.

"Like I mentioned before, my mama had a loan at the bank," she said after hesitating a minute. "We paid part of it with the last cotton we picked. But I don't think there's enough to pay the rest. And I don't know how to get any more money."

Henry nodded as he listened.

"Yep," he said, "money's hard ter come by when you ain't got none, dat's fo' sho'. But dere's ways er gittin' it."

"What ways?" asked Katie.

"Same ways you got it afore—jes' takes a mite longer, dat's all."

"What do you mean?"

"Well, we cud plant dose fields er yers wiff mo cotton nex' year, an' den dat cotton'd grow up an' up an' we cud pick it jes' like you done las' time, an' wiff me an' Jeremiah helpin', I figger you cud git hit in afore nex' year's rain."

"Could we . . . could we really plant more!" asked Katie excitedly. "How, Henry . . . when can we do it?"

Henry chuckled. "Well, jes' hold on ter yerse'f, Miz Kathleen," he said. "First we gots ter plough up dat ol' groun' an' we cudn't do dat till spring. Den you'd hab ter spend some er las' year's money fer seed from Mr. Watson. Den we cud plant it all right. Might take us er while. We ain't got dat macheenrey like I seen McSimmons usin'. But we cud do hit all right."

"When can we start!"

"We gots ter wait till spring, Miz Kathleen."

The minute Henry'd put the idea in Katie's head about planting and harvesting a new crop of cotton, her spirits rose and she couldn't wait for spring to come. Having that to look forward to made the fall and winter months go both faster and slower at the same time.

We'd been together now, the five of us, for more than half a year and gradually we were running out of things. We had to spend some of Katie's money in the bank for flour and sugar and other food, though we had more milk and cheese than we could eat.

We'd done some vegetable canning in the summer, but the flood destroyed what was left of the vegetable garden too. There were a lot of apples on the trees roundabout, so we went out picking and making and canning applesauce so we'd have it through the winter.

Henry helped us plant a new batch of potatoes and sweet potatoes with cut-up pieces from what we still had left over in the root cellar. And of course we kept making cheese and churning butter. And we had plenty of eggs.

Another thing we were running out of was meat. Katie mentioned this to Henry and his solution was simple enough.

"You got enuff hogs out dere—we'll butcher one ob dem, an' maybe one er yer cows too an' smoke an' cure an' salt it an' you'll hab plenty er meat fer winter."

"Ugh!" said Katie. "I don't think I could stand to watch."

Henry laughed. "You'd rather starve dan kill some ol' hog!"

"No, I don't suppose," said Katie. "It just sounds so horrible."

Katie's squeamishness didn't stop Henry. The very next week he came out planning to butcher one of the hogs.

"Do we have to watch, Uncle Henry?" asked Aleta.

"No, chil', you don' hab ter watch me kill it," said Henry. "But you two older girls," he added, looking at me and Katie, "you's gwine hab ter help me lift it into da pot. So you jes' fill yer biggest tub plumb full an' git a good hot fire aneath it, 'cause we gots ter hab boilin' water ter git a good scald on dat dere pig. You take care ob da fire an' I'll take care ob da killin', an' we'll hab dat ol' hog sliced an' hangin' in yer smokehouse an' in dat brine barrel in no time."

I was used to things like that, so I helped Henry most of the afternoon, and Aleta and Katie came and went as much as their stomachs could handle.

Aleta was gradually warming up to *Uncle Henry,* as she called him now. She was starting to grow like a weed. So was William! He was getting chubby and round, and even Emma was putting on a little weight. She was calming down too. Whenever Henry came to visit, Emma followed him around like a puppy dog, like she had Katie earlier. Henry was so kind and tender to her. I doubt if a man had ever been so kind to her, and Emma drank it in. She'd have done anything for Henry. For all I knew, she'd hardly known her father. Henry was just about as gentle a man as I'd ever seen. As kind as he was to all of us, you could tell he had a special place in his heart for Emma and William. Maybe it was because he knew they had no one else. And as the months passed, he became the father she'd never had.

Slowly the winter passed. There was more rain now and then, and it turned colder, but no more flooding.

A Visit and an Attack

13

One day a couple weeks before Christmas, late in the day, Jeremiah came to call. It had been a warm day and sunny and everything smelled wet and warm and nice. Jeremiah was all cleaned up and he had a sheepish look on his face when he came to the door. I knew immediately that he hadn't come to help us with our chores.

"How do, Miz Mayme," he said. "I thought . . . uh, maybe you an' me could go fer a walk."

I nodded and went outside with him.

We walked away from the house. Dusk was settling in. A huge full moon was just rising over the trees. It was just about as nice an evening as I could imagine. It was quiet as we walked. Neither of us seemed to have anything to say. He glanced around a few times, almost like he thought somebody else might be around or watching us, though I don't know who it could have been because Katie and the others were all still inside. Then he seemed to settle down and took my hand and we just kept walking and walking till we were in the woods by Katie's secret place and the house was out of sight. I wanted to show him the little meadow and to see what it was like in the moonlight, though I didn't want to without Katie's permission.

Gradually we started talking.

"What you gonna do now dat yer free?" Jeremiah asked. "You gonna keep working fer Miz Katie? You gonna work fo' her forever?"

"I don't know. I hadn't thought about it," I said. "But I could never leave Katie."

"Why not?"

"She's my friend."

"But she's white."

"She's like a sister to me. It doesn't matter what color she is."

"Seems ter me it matters. Whites an' blacks is different, ain't they?"

"Not down inside," I said. "Don't you figure if you could open us up, our hearts'd be the same color?"

"I don't know. I reckon I never thought 'bout dat."

"What about you?" I said. "What are you going to do?"

"I'd like ter save a little money," said Jeremiah enthusiastically, "an' maybe git me a livery er my own someday."

"That sounds like a fine idea, Jeremiah."

"My daddy's happy enuff ter work fer Mr. Guiness," he went on. "It's all he knows. He's pleased enuff ter hab a job an' ter be a free black man. But now dat young folks like you an' me is free, maybe we can do eben more—jes' think, a black man *owning* something. Don't it jes' soun' right fine!" His voice was excited as he thought about it.

"You can do it, Jeremiah," I said. "I know you will. But

I'm not ambitious like that. Besides, I'm just a girl. Girls can't do things like that."

"Why not? Maybe dey can . . . someday."

"Not colored girls."

"Why not? You's free, ain't you?"

"I reckon."

"Ain't nobody can tell you what you can an' can't do. So don't dat mean you can do whatever you want?"

"Maybe you're right. I just never thought about things like that before. Although Katie gave me twenty dollars an' that almost makes me feel like I could do anything."

"Twenty dollars!" exclaimed Jeremiah. "Ob yer very own . . . real money!"

"Yep. It's in the bank in town with my own name on it."

"Why, yer rich, Mayme!"

I laughed. I guess it shows how used to Katie's kindness I'd already become.

We walked on and finally turned around. It was pretty well dark by now. It was such a nice contented feeling walking along, with the moon shining down on us, hand in hand, knowing we were really *free* people. Was this how it had always been for white girls when they got to this age, meeting a boy and feeling things inside and then having him take your hand and treat you like you were special?

I found myself thinking about my mama and wondering how it had been when she'd first met my papa and wondering if she'd fallen in love slowly like I thought I might be doing right now, or if she and he'd been brought together by Master McSimmons without any choice in the matter. I hoped my mama and daddy had been in love. I hoped I was a child of love. But since they were both dead, I reckoned I'd never know.

But then Jeremiah's voice interrupted my thoughts, and his words were the last ones I'd expected to hear.

"You ever think . . . about gittin' married?" he asked after it had been quiet three or four minutes.

I felt the heat immediately rising in my neck. I was glad it was dark.

"I reckon," I said softly. "Doesn't everybody?" I suppose I had been thinking about it just then, since I'd been thinking about my mama and daddy.

"But hit's different now, you know," Jeremiah went on. "Wiff no masters tellin' us what we gotta do. Now we can make up our own minds who to marry an' what we wants ter do."

We were coming out of the woods now and into the clearing of fields and open space. The moon made everything glow a pale silver. I don't know what I'd have said, but I didn't have the chance.

Suddenly we heard voices yelling.

"There he is!" shouted a voice. You could tell it was white.

"Look—he's got a nigger girl with him!" yelled another one. "Let's get them!"

I felt Jeremiah's arm tense as he turned toward the shouts. It filled me with terror to know he was afraid.

"Who is it!" I said.

"Jes' some no goods dat follered me from town. I thought I'd got dem off my trail.—You run, Mayme. You git back to da house an' you an' Miz Kathleen, you lock dem doors!"

"But, Jeremiah, what about—"

"You go, Mayme.—Go now!"

Too afraid not to do what he said, I turned and ran for the house.

"There she goes—after her!" shouted one of the white boys.

I looked back. I saw them now, coming at us from the middle of the pasture next to the road. One of them tore off from the others toward me. I kept running as fast as I could, but he was a lot faster and in just a few seconds had nearly caught me. I screamed.

Then out of the corner of my eye I saw a dark figure rush at him and knock him over, and they both thudded to the ground with grunts and sounds of fighting.

"Why, you cussed nigger!" the white boy yelled in a fury. "I'll kill you for that if I—"

But Jeremiah silenced him with a whack of his fist. I tried to keep running but couldn't help looking back. The others quickly caught up and knocked Jeremiah off their friend and started pounding and beating him something fierce.

I felt my eyes getting hot and wet, but I knew I could do nothing to help him. I had to keep going. A few seconds later I ran into the kitchen.

"They've got Jeremiah!" I cried. "Oh, Katie, there's some white boys out there and they're beating him up and I'm afraid they're going to kill him!"

Katie was getting more and more gumption all the time, that was for sure. Sometimes she amazed me. This time she didn't even think twice about it. I had hardly got the words out when she ran into the parlor and came back holding one of her papa's shotguns. Now it was my frightened eyes that got wide.

"Katie, he told me to lock the doors," I said. But she was walking straight to the door.

"We're not going to let them kill him," she said.

"But what if they—"

"As long as I'm holding this, they're not going to hurt me," she said. "Mayme, go get me one of my daddy's hats out of the pantry while I'm loading this. Maybe they'll think I'm a man, or if nothing else my mama. I'm not going to let what happened to you happen to Jeremiah."

Five seconds later she walked outside with as determined a look in her eyes as I'd ever seen, with one of her papa's big wide-brimmed hats flopping down over her face so you couldn't quite tell how old she was. She was wearing a long work dress, so I don't think anyone was going to mistake her for her daddy. But a woman could pull a trigger just as well as a man. I guess she'd fought hard enough by now to save Rosewood that she was starting to think like she was its master and mistress all in one. And I reckon she was!

She walked out and along the road. It wasn't hard to tell where they were. She could hear the sounds of scuffling and swearing and fighting. She walked about halfway toward the commotion, then let the first barrel go. The sudden explosion brought the fight to an abrupt halt. There were only three of them. They stopped and looked up from where they were kicking and pounding on Jeremiah where he lay on the ground. Katie kept marching straight toward them.

"All right, you've had your fun!" she yelled in her Mrs. Clairborne voice. "Now get out of here before I use this again. If I have to go get my husband to see to you thugs, he won't be none too happy."

"He's just a nigger, lady," said one of them, slowly climbing off Jeremiah's chest. "We was just having some fun."

"Well, have your fun someplace else. Now get out of here!"

Muttering and swearing, the three started wandering away.

"You can move faster than that!" yelled Katie.

They started running slowly in the direction of town. When they were about fifty yards away, I heard another shot. This time I think she was aiming at them because they started yelling like they were mad and scared all at once and tore off and were soon out of sight.

I ran out to join Katie and we hurried to Jeremiah.

He was lying on the ground moaning and groaning. He sounded bad.

"Jeremiah . . . Jeremiah," I said, kneeling down to him. "How bad is it?"

"I's be all right," he moaned. "I think one ob my ribs is broken, but dat ain't too bad."

"Can you stand up?"

"I don't know . . . I reckon."

We helped him to his feet. Then holding on to both of us, with his arms around our shoulders and with Katie still lugging the shotgun, we got him to the house. Once we were inside, with the light from the lantern, I had to turn away. Jeremiah's face was bloody and swollen and I could tell he was hurting real bad. But Katie wasn't queasy and was already tending to him with a wet cloth. Of course

Emma immediately went into a babbling fit. We washed him up as best we could and then got him to the couch in the parlor.

"You're spending the night here, Jeremiah," said Katie. "You could never get back to town tonight. And I'm worried about those white boys. I'll ride into town and get your daddy in the morning as soon as it's light."

He didn't argue. We tried to get him to eat and drink something, but he was hurting too bad to eat and fell asleep soon after that.

We did lock the doors, like he'd told us to, and Katie kept the gun loaded all night. But there was no more trouble.

The Winter Passes

14

JEREMIAH WAS IN BAD SHAPE THE NEXT MORNING. He tried to be brave like men always do, but you could tell he was in a lot of pain. One eye was swollen shut and there were great bloody welts all over his face. And he could hardly move or turn over from the broken ribs.

Katie was back with Henry by midmorning. There wasn't much Henry could do for Jeremiah either. After he hadn't come home the night before, Henry was relieved that he was all right but pained to see him in such a state. We decided Jeremiah should stay at Rosewood another day or two, at least until some of the soreness had subsided enough that he could walk and get on a horse.

Katie wanted to take him to Doc Carter.

"I don't care what it costs," she said. "I'll take the money out of the bank."

But Henry wouldn't hear of it.

"I don' want ter arouse no talk," he said. "Doc's a good

man, but he's da white folks' doc an' I don' want no talk 'bout dis. Dere's too much goin' on dese days, too many beatin's an' hangin's. I don' want ter rile nobody. Da bes' we can do is ter let dis drop an' jes' keep quiet 'bout it."

Katie finally saw that he was right, and gradually Jeremiah got back to normal without the doc's help.

The new year of 1866 came, and Katie was more anxious than ever to get to planting. But Henry kept saying it wasn't time yet and that we had to be patient.

By late February the weather was slowly starting to turn warmer and Henry came out and ploughed one field. He told us what to ask for when we went to Mr. Watson's to buy seed, which we did, coming home with several big bags on the back of the wagon.

We got one field planted, and Henry and Jeremiah got to work on ploughing another. Now all we could do was wait till the cotton grew up and then we'd pick it again. Unfortunately, events weren't so patient and didn't wait for the cotton.

When we were alone, Katie and I still sometimes talked about what we were going to do with Aleta.

Once Katie said to her, "Aleta, we've got to find your father. Don't you want to go back and live with him?"

"No."

"But why?"

"I'm afraid of him. He's the reason my mother got killed."

Katie and I looked at each other but didn't correct her. Perhaps, indirectly, Aleta's father *was* responsible, but it still seemed like someday we had to find out who he was. And so we kept going and didn't know what to do except keep her with us for a while longer. We had the feeling Henry knew more than he'd let on about Aleta and her father, and I couldn't help remembering what Reverend Hall had said to Katie. But we weren't sure what was the right thing to do.

In the middle of April, Katie's world suddenly crashed when another letter arrived from the bank.

To Rosalind Clairborne, it said,

> *As you know, your second loan is due and payable next month. While foreclosure proceedings were halted last September with your payment of the first loan, I am afraid the bank will not be able to grant an extension on this present balance. There is pressure from New York to make sure all accounts are kept current. As a reminder, as I am certain your records will confirm, the balance due is $350. I hope to hear from you soon.*
>
> *Yours very truly,*
> *M. Taylor, Greens Crossing Bank*

Katie put down the letter with a look of disbelief on her face.

"I think we'd better take the cotton in the barn to sell," she said. "We can't wait any longer, whatever the price is."

The next day we hitched up two teams of two horses to the two wagons that had been sitting in the barn all winter. By now Emma and Aleta were enough used to things that Katie's and my leaving for a few hours wasn't so fearsome for them, though we still took our usual precautions in case anyone came.

Mr. Watson seemed a little surprised to see us as we pulled up in front of his mill, though I thought either Katie or Henry had told him we had more cotton to sell. He looked it over as if he didn't like the looks of it too much, then had his men unload it and take it inside to weigh it while we waited. Katie was really nervous. She had her heart set on this cotton getting her the money she needed. I guess I was nervous too, but not like Katie. Actually, since I knew he made deliveries for Mr. Watson, I was thinking more about Jeremiah than the price of cotton and was looking around to see if he was there.

"Well, Kathleen," said Mr. Watson when he walked out of the mill, "I don't have real good news for your mama. Some of the load must have gotten wet because there was some mildew around the edges. And the price is down right now. I'm afraid all I can give her is eleven cents a pound."

Katie nodded as she listened. "And, uh . . . how much does it come to, Mr. Watson?" she asked.

"It came out to six hundred sixty-five pounds, which came to seventy-three dollars. I wish it was more, but I'm afraid that's the best I can do."

I saw Katie's face go pale at the words "seventy-three dollars." I knew she had been hoping for three times that much.

She took the money, but as soon as she began walking back to where I was standing by the wagons I saw tears filling her eyes.

"It's not enough, Mayme," she said. "It's not enough. What are we going to do?"

We walked down the street to the bank in silence. Katie put the money into her mother's account. She had taken a little more out of it through the winter, and with what she'd used for the seed, it now totaled one hundred eighty-seven dollars. That was a hundred sixty-three dollars less than the loan.

Katie was right. It wasn't enough.

Overheard Plans
15

A week or two later, Henry was working in the livery stalls one morning. Three men came in to saddle their horses. He hadn't been there when they'd dropped them off earlier and said he didn't know any of them. They didn't know he was there.

As soon as he heard them start talking, Henry's ears perked up and he stopped still so he could listen and so they wouldn't hear him.

". . . say we go out there again," one of the men said.

"The way I hear it," said the second man, "Clairborne ain't ever coming back from the war."

". . . think he's dead?" asked the third.

"Ain't no telling . . ."

". . . lots of men . . . still missing. Maybe some of them just don't want to come back."

"All I know is that if it's just the woman and her kid and a colored brat, what's to stop us?"

". . . still don't get us Ward . . ."

"We been up and down the state looking . . . every clue points right back here . . . gotta be there . . . should have tossed the place last time . . ."

". . . think that fancy-talking brother of his knows something . . . should've pressed him harder."

"Doubt he knows . . ."

". . . a yellow coward . . . he'd a talked if we pressed him harder . . . lost track of him too."

". . . what'd Sneed say?"

". . . go out tomorrow and nose around . . ."

By then the men were about done and started leading their horses out and that was all Henry heard.

He knew they were talking about Rosewood and Katie's papa, and he recognized the name Sneed from being in Oakwood occasionally. He said he didn't like the sound of the men's voices. It sounded to him like we might be in some kind of danger.

He snuck out and watched the men leave. Right then they were going in the opposite direction from Rosewood, so he went back to his work. But from the sound of it, they were planning on paying us another visit real soon.

Henry worked hard to finish up his work that day, then told the livery owner that he was leaving for a day or two. Mr. Guiness asked him what for, but Henry said he couldn't say. Mr. Guiness wasn't none too happy about it, Henry said, but since Henry was determined, there wasn't much he could do about it.

We saw Henry late that same afternoon. He walked into the barn just as Katie and I were finishing up the evening milking.

"Aftahnoon t' you ladies," he said. "Dere's some biz'ness I gotter discuss wiff you."

Henry's expression was more serious than usual. A worried look came over Katie's face.

Aleta wasn't there, which I was glad of. Henry pulled up a stool and sat down and told us what he'd heard that morning.

"Why'd dose three men be comin' here?" he asked.

"They were here once before," said Katie.

"Why's dat?"

Katie looked over at me, and I know she was wondering whether she should tell Henry about her uncle and the gold coins she'd found in his trousers in the cellar.

"They were looking for my uncle," she finally answered.

"Dat uncle you don' want ter go live wif?"

"No, my uncle that went to California and who's dead now."

Henry nodded slowly.

"Well," he said after a bit, "I'm thinkin' dat maybe I oughter jes' stay wiff y'all fer a spell, an' sleep in da barn here agin, maybe jes' a night er two. We'll see what happens, jes' ter make sure dey don' mean no harm. I jes' didn't like da soun' er dose men."

Katie nodded and said that would be fine.

Temporary Boarder at Rosewood

16

HENRY'D BEEN AROUND SO MUCH THROUGH the winter that his staying with us for a while didn't seem like that big a change from normal. I think we all slept a little better knowing he was down in the barn. We'd been taking care of ourselves for so long we'd stopped even thinking about it. But having Henry there made us realize all over again that we were just girls, not grown-ups. Even if Henry was black and just cleaned stalls and took care of horses in Greens Crossing, he *was* a grown-up. And he was a *man* too, and a big strong one. If something was to happen, he could do things we couldn't.

By the time I got up and went outside the next morning, Henry already had half the cows milked. He was sitting there whistling softly to himself, looking like he was having the time of his life. He heard me come into the barn and turned around.

"Mo'nin', Miz Mayme—y'all sleep well?"

"Yes," I said.

Being alone with Henry reminded me that we were both black, and both here sort of making ourselves at home on a white man's plantation. I guess Henry must have been thinking along the same lines.

"Dis place be a powerful lot er work," said Henry. "You an' da others keepin' up wiff da milkin' an' da other chores?"

"Yes," I said. "Even Emma's learning to work real hard, just like Katie did. Katie could hardly do anything at first, and now she works just as hard as me . . . and chases off white boys with a shotgun."

Henry chuckled. "Yep," he nodded, "I sure wish I cud er seen dat! Soun's like you's right proud er her."

"I reckon I am," I said. "Do you really think those men'll come, Henry?"

"I do, Miz Mayme," he said. "Dey sounded mighty set on hit."

"You want some help with the milking?" I asked.

"I'm nearly done wiff hit."

"I reckon I'll go inside, then, and help Katie with the breakfast."

I turned to go, but then Henry spoke up again.

"You min' effen I ax you a question, Miz Mayme?" he said.

"No . . . of course not."

"What it be like sleepin' dere in da big house?"

I hesitated for a second, wondering if he was hinting that it was wrong of me. But from the look on his face, I realized that he was just curious. Even though he'd been free before the war, the idea of such a thing as I was doing had never occurred to him.

"Just like anywhere else, I reckon," I said, "once you get used to it."

"Wuz it yer idea, at first, I mean—after you foun' Miz Kathleen?"

"Oh no. I was going to sleep in here, like you're doing. I was terrified at the thought of anyone knowing I'd slept in a white man's bed."

Henry laughed at the thought.

"But Katie wanted me to stay with her. She was so helpless at first I didn't think I ought to leave her alone."

"Don' it make you feel a mite all overish?" Henry asked.

"It did for a while," I said. "At first I slept on the floor, but then she made me sleep in one of the beds, and I could hardly sleep for fear of what would happen if somebody found me. I knew I'd get the tar whipped outta me. But I reckon I got used to it. Katie's been awful good to me."

"Soun's ter me dat you's helped her some considerable yo'self. Seems ter me she was a bit on da helpless side a year back."

"I reckon you're right," I said. "She was in a bad way when I came. She could hardly do anything for herself. But look at her now. And like I said, even Emma's learning how to do things too."

"I reckon takin' care ob yersel' makes a body learn what he's got ter do all right."

It got quiet a minute.

"You bury 'em?" Henry asked. "Miz Kathleen's kin?"

"Yes, sir."

Henry nodded.

"Well . . .'peers ter me you done right well by both ob 'em. Miz Kathleen's lookin' better'n I eber seen her. She's done growed up a mite. I reckon dat's why I started noticin' da two er you in town, seein' somefin different in Miz Kathleen's face dat I cudn't esplain ter mysel'. An' now I'm seein' dat same growin'-up look in Miz Emma. Yep . . . you gots lots ter be proud ob, Miz Mayme. You done real good by dem."

"Thank you, Henry," I said. "Well . . . I reckon I'll go get started on that breakfast. You'll probably be hungry."

Later that morning Katie and I talked about what we should do if the men came like Henry thought they would. I said I thought we should do our same plan with fires burning and laundry hanging out.

"I've been thinking, Mayme," said Katie, "that I could dress up and pretend to be my mama."

"What!" I laughed. But then I saw that Katie was downright serious. "Do you really think you could?" I asked.

"I fooled those boys that were beating up Jeremiah."

"But it was dark . . . and you had a gun!"

"I'll just wear old clothes and a scarf or hat or something, and you could smear some dust or dirt on my face, like I'd been cleaning or something, so that it would be harder to tell how young I was."

"That's some kind of crazy notion," I laughed. "But if anyone can do it, it's Kathleen Clairborne!"

"Should we tell Henry?" said Katie.

"I don't know," I said.

"What do you think he'd say?"

"Something tells me he might not like it," I said. "I

don't think he'd be too fond of us not telling the truth."

"Then we won't tell him," said Katie. "I'll just go upstairs and get dressed, and if he asks you tell him I'm in my room. After a while you come up and help me try to look right."

"What will we do when the men come?"

"You and Aleta go about your business outside. We'll keep Emma and William in one of the bedrooms. And I'll watch for them from upstairs."

"What about Henry?"

"We'll just hope they think he's a hired black man. All we need is for them to see him so they know there's men around."

"Not *men,* Miss Katie—just one man."

"One man's better than we've had up till now."

The Men
17

IT WAS RIGHT AFTER LUNCH WHEN THE MEN CAME. Henry was cleaning up inside the barn at the time. I reckon he figured there wasn't anything else for him to be doing, so he might as well help us out how he could. Already the barn was looking tidier than I'd ever seen it.

We heard them coming, so we quickly jumped to our plan. Katie sent Aleta out the door where she could sneak down to the cabins and light the fires we'd laid. I adjusted Katie's hair and scarf and tried to muss up her face one last time, then she went upstairs to wait. Then I headed out into the yard to hang out the laundry. I was just starting when they rode around the barn and up to the house. I hoped they wouldn't notice that the clothes I was hanging up were already dry!

I tried not to pay them much attention as they rode past me. After they were around to the front of the house, I ran into the barn.

"Henry . . . Henry," I whispered, "they're here." But I

could tell he'd heard them too.

"Where's Miz Kathleen?" he said, hurrying over to me.

"She's in the house. She'll talk to them. But maybe you should just walk around outside so they see you and know there's a man around."

"What 'bout Miz Kathleen?"

"She'll be all right," I said.

We went out of the barn together and saw Aleta already headed back from the cabins. I thought to myself, *Don't hurry, Aleta . . . just keep looking like it's nothing unusual!*

I could hear them banging on the front door, then pretty soon a couple of them rode around to the back door by the kitchen since nobody'd answered in front.

It didn't look too good—three rough white men, a colored girl hiding with her baby inside, scared out of her wits, a white girl inside the house dressed up like her mama, a little white girl coming through the fields, and Henry standing there with me watching it all and starting to get a confused look on his face, since he didn't know anything about how we'd been dealing with people who came visiting.

By now the men were banging at the back door, and one of them was calling out. They hadn't paid any attention to Henry or me. Most of the time it seemed like white folks didn't even notice us coloreds.

Finally Katie stuck her head out the upstairs window.

"Hello," she said down toward the men. "What can I do for you gentlemen?"

The men looked up at her. And Henry looked up at her too, and his eyes were about as big as Katie's all of a sudden when he saw her looking so different and trying to make her voice low so she would sound like a grown-up. But there was one person who wasn't looking up at Katie, and that was me! I couldn't have looked right then, but I was sure listening!

"You be Mrs. Clairborne, ma'am?" said one of them. His voice sounded a little uncertain, like he wasn't quite sure what to make of the face that had appeared in the upstairs window of the house.

"Yes, sir, that's right."

"Your husband back from the war, ma'am?" he asked.

"Yes, he is," answered Katie. "He got back two months ago."

"Could I talk to him, then?"

"I am sorry, but he is out in the woods with the men and one of the wagons getting some timbers."

Katie paused and looked at me.

"Mayme, pump some fresh water for their horses."

"Yes'm," I said and turned slowly away.

"Is there something I can help you with?" asked Katie. As I went I saw Henry out of the corner of my eye standing there dumbfounded. The three men looked as confused as him, but then two of them led the three horses to the trough while the third one stood there and kept talking to Katie.

"No, I reckon there ain't," he said. "When do you expect him back?"

"About any time now," Katie answered, glancing in the direction of the woods. "Don't you think so, Henry? He and the other men ought to be back soon?"

Henry just stared back at her, then mumbled something

that could have meant just about anything, but the man seemed to take it as a yes.

One of them wandered back from the water trough and the two men talked between themselves for a bit. I couldn't hear anything, but they looked a little mystified about how this was turning out. Then one of them looked up toward Katie again.

"Word has it, ma'am," he said, "that he's got him a brother-in-law who was out west for a spell—that be your brother, ma'am?"

"That's right . . . my brother Ward. Are you friends of his?"

"In a manner of speaking, ma'am. We're trying to get in touch with him, and it's a matter of some importance. . . . If you could tell us where he is, ma'am, we'd be much obliged."

"I would like to help you," said Katie. "But I'm afraid I haven't seen or heard from my brother in years.—I am sorry, but I'm going to have to ask you to excuse me. We've been passing a sickness around that's very contagious, and I'm feeling faint. I think I need to go lie down. Good day, gentlemen."

Katie pulled her head back inside and everything got quiet for a minute. The men kind of stood there looking at each other, not knowing quite what to do. There was nobody left to talk to but Henry standing over by the barn and me where I'd gone back to the laundry. And they didn't seem too inclined to talk to either of us. Aleta was just wandering up too, but they didn't pay any more attention to her than they had to me.

Finally they got back on their horses and rode away real

slow, like they still didn't know what to make of it all.

I glanced over at Henry. He still stood looking up at the empty window where Katie had been. Then he glanced over at me where I was pretending to be hanging the laundry, then down toward the slave cabins where smoke was now rising in the air from the fires Aleta had started, then finally back to where the men on their horses were just disappearing around the side of the barn.

"Well, if dat ain't da beatenest thing I eber saw!" he finally mumbled to himself.

A Talk With Henry
18

When it was all over, Henry came inside and sat down. Katie was still made up to look older, and Emma and Aleta were laughing. But Henry had a serious look on his face.

"I reckon hit's time you all tol' me a little more er what's goin' on roun' here," he said.

His tone silenced us. Henry was such a peaceable and loving man, just one look from him was enough. I didn't know much about such things yet, but later in my life when I understood a little more about how God works, I reckon what I'd say is that his looks could be convicting to your spirit.

That's the kind of man Henry was. He knew when one of us was feeling down or sad, and a smile or the gentle touch of his rough hand on your cheek, or a squeeze round your shoulder in reassurance from his big strong arm was enough to make you know you were loved and that everything was going to be all right. But a stern look was enough to send a knife into your heart too. But a good knife. Cutting out bad things from inside you's a good and necessary thing, and if it sometimes takes a little pain to get it done, I reckon that's the price a person has to pay to grow up and become the kind of person God wants him to be—or who God wants *her* to be. A lot of folks don't spend a lot of time thinking about who God wants them to be—they just spend their lives being who *they* want to be. And I can't say I was thinking too much about it yet at that time. I was only sixteen. But I was starting to think about it, and having Henry around helped me think about it more because I kind of had the feeling that when he looked at me it was almost like God looking at me, and it made me think about things a mite different.

I'm sure most of the white folks who'd known Henry for years just looked at him and saw a quiet colored man who couldn't speak as well as them, and who couldn't even read, and took him for an ignorant man. That's the trouble with people of all colors—they judge folks by what they think they see, which is usually only on the outside. But it's what's inside that counts. That's what makes a person who he or she really is. And sometimes it takes a little work to dig down inside and see what someone's made of, what kind of stuff their character has in it. That's just about one of the most important things in life—learning how to do that, learning how to find out what people are made of.

Henry was a man who I had the feeling had been doing that most of his life. You could tell his eyes saw things that other people didn't see, probably from spending so much time in his mind with God.

Henry had a saying that he said every once in a while

that he said explained a lot about life. It was that the color of your skin ain't the color of your heart. Then he'd say that the color of your heart was the most important thing in all of life. Was it dark and full of mean and selfish and unkind things? Or was your heart light and pink and warm and full of kind and unselfish things? Someday, he said, maybe not till we died, everything that was on the outside would fall away, and what color your skin was and where you lived and what people thought about you and how much money you had . . . none of that would matter because no one would see it anymore. The only thing they would be able to see was the color of your heart. Some hearts would be ugly and dark, and others would be warm and light and full of love. It wouldn't matter what color your skin was then.

So on this day, as he looked around at all of us, I knew Henry was looking to see what color our hearts were.

"Uh . . . what do you mean, Henry?" said Katie after a minute.

"Jes' dat I know you been all alone here an' dat you been doin' some pretendin' ter git by. But effen dese ol' ears ain't mistaken, I heard you say some things dat weren't true, Miz Kathleen. An' I ain't sayin' hit's right or wrong what you done, 'cuz I don' know all dere is ter know, an' dat's da Lord's job ter divide atween right an' wrong an' not mine, nohow. But I's jes' tryin' ter git a grip on what color yer heart is in all dese strange goin's-on."

It was silent a minute. I knew Katie felt just the same as me about Henry. As determined as she could be sometimes, and as grown-up as she'd gotten about making decisions and running off rowdy white boys, she could be as tender as a little girl too. I reckon she and me and Emma were still little girls down inside, and yet halfway to becoming grown-up women at the same time. And sometimes it was confusing not knowing which one was making you feel the things you felt—the girl or the woman.

Right now the little girl in Katie came to the surface from Henry's words, and she started to cry.

"I don't know either, Henry," she said softly, sniffling and wiping at her eyes and nose. "When Mayme and I first started, we talked about it some, and we knew lying was wrong, but we didn't know what else to do. It started one day when Mr. Thurston came by and I just couldn't tell him about what had happened. I was afraid. And then after that, we just kept telling people that my mama was still alive and that my daddy wasn't home yet."

"What wuz you afraid ob, chil'?"

"That they'd take me away, that my uncle Burchard would come and take Rosewood, that they'd hurt Mayme."

"Yep," said Henry like he did, nodding and thinking as he said it. "Yep . . . I kin see dat, all right. You wuz feared fer Miz Mayme."

"Yes," said Katie. "She practically saved my life. I couldn't let anything happen to her."

"Wuz you feared fer yerse'f?"

"I suppose . . . yes, I was afraid for myself too. I didn't know what they might do to me. I didn't want them to take me away someplace."

"Yep . . . yep," nodded Henry slowly. "I kin see dat it was a sore difficult thing, all right. 'Peers t' me dat da color er yer heart wuz good enuff. You wuzn't tryin' ter do nobody no harm, an' I can't see dat no harm's been done. An' it don't 'pear t' me dat dose men was up ter no good, an' so maybe what you done was right. But now we gots ter ax da Lord 'bout all dis."

He looked around at the rest of us, then opened his big arms and drew us all together as much as he could. We put our arms around each other, and then Henry started to pray.

"Dear Lord," he said, "we's yer chilluns, an' we's tryin' our bes' ter figger out how t' be good chilluns, but sometimes hit's a mite hard, Lord. We know dat lyin's wrong, but den Miz Kathleen an' Miz Mayme's been in some kind er difficult predikament here an' dey's jes' tryin' ter protect dereselves an' Miz Aleta an' Miz Emma an' her little boy from what folks might do effen dey foun' out. But, Lord, da truf's gotta come out sometime, an' so we ax you what's right ter be done an' ter show us what you want us ter do 'bout it all."

Henry gave us all a hug when he was through, then he left to go back to town. He said he would try to come back as soon as he could and would let us know if he found out anything more about the men.

Katie Gets Desperate

19

I woke up one morning, and when I went downstairs I was surprised to see the carpet pulled back and the trapdoor into the cellar open. I saw the light from a lantern and heard noise coming up from below.

I got down on my knees and poked my head in.

There was Katie down in the cellar with a shovel in her hand, sleeves rolled up, dirt on her hands and face, and sweating like she'd been working down there for hours. The chest where we'd found the gold coins in her uncle's trousers was shoved to one side, and all the things inside it were strewn about on the dirt floor. And there were holes all about the cellar where she had apparently been digging.

"Katie," I said as I climbed down, "what are you doing!"

The lantern she'd brought down was flickering like it was about out of oil. I noticed the old brass lantern she'd tried to move that other time and wondered why she hadn't lit it, since it was bigger.

Katie looked up at me but kept right on digging.

"It's got to be here!" she said.

"What does?"

"The gold . . . there's got to be more gold! I know my uncle had more gold than just those few coins."

Whack went the shovel again into the hard dirt. But she was hardly scooping much out. The floor was so dry and hard packed, and Katie was obviously exhausted.

"How long have you been down here?" I asked.

"I don't know," said Katie in a weary voice. "A few hours. I couldn't sleep from worrying about the money and Rosewood and what's going to happen."

"Why don't you take a rest. Come up and let's have some breakfast and then we can talk about it."

"I don't want to talk about it!" she snapped. "And I don't want any breakfast. I want to find the gold! We've got to pay back the bank."

She looked at me and her eyes were flashing. I'd never seen a look like it in Katie's face before. It was as if the idea of the gold had possessed her.

She went on trying to dig the hole deeper.

"Do you think it might be . . . there?" I asked. "Right there? Is that why you're digging that hole?"

"That's what people do, don't they?" she said. "They bury gold in the ground." She threw another small shovelful of dirt onto the pile beside the hole.

"But why . . . right *there*?" I asked again. "What made you think to start digging right there?"

Katie stopped and her hands were trembling. Then I saw her eyes filling with tears. The shovel fell from her hands with a thud and she nearly collapsed on the dirt floor.

"Oh, Mayme . . . I don't know!" she wailed. "Nothing made me start digging here, I just did. I don't know why. There's no reason it should be here . . . I just had to do something. I just looked through the chest, and then moved it away and started digging. It might just as well be over under that potato barrel in the corner. It's stupid . . . I'm stupid for thinking of such a thing. I just . . . I just don't know what to do! And I'm so worried they'll take Rosewood from us!"

She began to sob and sat there with her dirty hands in her face and tears pouring down her cheeks.

I knelt beside her and wrapped my arms around her. Katie sobbed and sobbed. If she had really been up half the night, no wonder she was exhausted and her emotions were worn to a frazzle.

We sat there for a long time and I let her cry.

"Why don't we go upstairs," I said. "You can get cleaned up and have something to eat and maybe take a bath and a nap. You'll feel better after a bath and some sleep."

Katie didn't argue. I helped her to her feet and toward the steps. I could tell she was completely spent. I doubted whether she'd even make it through breakfast and a bath before falling asleep.

But before I could even get her back up out of the cellar, suddenly Emma's head appeared in the opening above our heads.

"You better come up quick," she said. "Dat man's here agin."

Surprise Visitor
20

EMMA'S WORDS SENT A CHILL THROUGH ME. Whoever she meant I didn't know, but visitors around here were not usually a welcome sight.

I helped Katie up the stairs and then followed her, carrying the lantern she'd brought down with her. I handed it up to Emma and then climbed the last few steps up into the parlor.

In the doorway to the kitchen stood Templeton Daniels.

"My, my!" he said in that humorous voice of his. "This is quite a sight! What were you looking for down there—buried treasure!"

Then he looked at me, and all the humor and wittiness went out of his expression. He got the oddest, most serious look on his face. It was almost like there was something inside him he was trying to say but couldn't get out.

"Hello, Mayme," he said after a second or two. His voice was quiet, strange, calm, completely different than how he'd spoken to Katie. He held my eyes with his just a second . . . and then smiled, almost nervously, I thought.

"Uncle Templeton," said Katie, breaking the strange spell in the air that had even temporarily silenced Emma. "What a surprise—what are you doing here?"

Again an odd look passed over her uncle's face, and again came a smile. "Let's just say I left a little suddenly last time, and that I had some unfinished business here I needed to take care of."

He looked better than the last time we had seen him, better groomed and his clothes cleaner. He didn't look like he was trying to hide from someone like I'd thought last time. I got the idea he had come, strange as it was to say it . . . because he actually *wanted* to see us.

"What kind of business?" asked Katie.

"Never mind about that right now. Let's just say that I need to have a long talk with the two of you—"

As he said it he glanced over at me. I couldn't imagine what he wanted to talk to *me* about, unless he had decided what to do about Katie's future and wanted me to know about it.

"—There's plenty of time for all that," he went on. "But what's all this?" he added. "You look like you've been prospecting, Kathleen."

"Oh, Uncle Templeton," said Katie, "the bank's going to take Rosewood away if we don't pay back my mama's loan, and there's not enough money and the rain ruined the cotton and I was looking for Uncle Ward's gold!"

Mr. Daniels took in Katie's flood of information with a thoughtful nod.

"You know, Kathleen," he said after a moment, "I spent

the night in your barn out there and I'm hungry and could use a cup or two of good strong coffee. So why don't we see what we can find in here to eat, and then we'll talk about it."

Almost the same moment, a cry sounded from William upstairs and Emma ran off to tend to him. Then Aleta's steps came bounding down the stairs but stopped abruptly when she saw Katie's uncle standing there.

While Katie was explaining it all to Aleta, I went into the kitchen, stoked up the fire, put on some water to boil, and got out some bread and milk and cheese and eggs for breakfast.

"Why did you sleep in the barn?" Katie was asking as she and Aleta and Mr. Daniels came into the kitchen.

"I didn't get here until late, Kathleen," he said. "I didn't want to bother you young ladies, or frighten you. So I just snuck into the barn as quietly as I could."

"Did you sleep well?"

"It wasn't exactly the sort of accommodations I'm used to," he laughed, "but I managed to doze off. But tell me, do cows and horses *ever* sleep? It seemed I heard them moving and shuffling and snorting all night long!"

"I don't know, Uncle Templeton."

Ten minutes later we were all seated at the table and I had just poured Mr. Daniels some coffee. He took the steaming cup in his hands and put his nose to it almost like the smell was better than drinking it. "That smells mighty fine, Mayme," he said, looking up at me with a smile. "Thank you."

"Do you know where it is, Uncle Templeton?" said Katie as she munched on a piece of buttered bread. "Did

Uncle Ward or Mama tell you what he did with his gold?"

"Well, your mama, God rest her soul, knew me well enough, I'm sorry to say, *not* to tell me anything about it," he answered, sipping at the cup. "That is, if she knew anything herself. And Ward and I weren't exactly on the best of terms when he disappeared, so you can be sure *he* never told me anything. So I don't even know if there is any gold, Kathleen," he added with a sigh. "And that's the truth. All I know is that there are some men who think there is, and they've been hounding me for a year trying to get on Ward's trail."

"Yes . . . those must be the same men who came here looking for him!"

A concerned look came over his face.

"When?" he asked.

"Twice," answered Katie. "Once a year ago, and then again just last week."

"They know about Rosewood. . . . You mean *those* are the men you chased off with guns?!"

Katie nodded.

"Hmm . . . that's not good. They didn't . . . do anything—hurt any of you?" said Mr. Daniels, glancing around at the rest of us, still looking serious.

"No—we fooled them and they left."

"Well, they're likely to be back. They don't give up easily. It's taken me a long time to shake them loose. I made the mistake of tangling with one of them once in a poker game too, and that didn't help. I'm afraid I took him for quite a bit of money. It sure won't do for them to find me here. That will make it bad for all of us. They're sure to think something's up then, and it will put you in even more danger than you are now."

"But what about the gold, Uncle Templeton?" persisted Katie. "What about the gold!" That same desperate sound had come back into her voice that she'd had down in the basement. I thought she was going to start crying again.

Mr. Daniels let out a long sigh.

"I don't know, Kathleen," he said. "For a long time I was convinced that Ward had struck it big in California too. But now I'm not so sure. Your ma wouldn't have let the place run down if she could help it. A lot of tales of gold got spun in California. And I imagine a few of them were true. But a lot more weren't. More men lost their lives trying to get rich than got rich. Most of the tales are just that—tales . . . stories without much truth in them. To make a long story short, Kathleen, I don't think Ward had any gold."

"Then what are we going to do, Uncle Templeton?" said Katie in a forlorn voice. "What are we going to *do*! We can't let them take Rosewood away."

It was obvious by now that Katie was too tired even to cry. Her eyelids were drooping. Sitting down and having something to eat had made her so drowsy she was about to fall asleep right at the table.

"Katie," I said, "why don't we get you cleaned up and you can take a nap and then you can talk to your uncle later."

"A good idea!" said Mr. Daniels, finishing off the last of the coffee in his cup. "Nobody's going to take Rosewood from us today, and we'll have plenty of time to talk later and try to figure out what's to be done. In the meantime, I'll bring my things in. Actually, I could use a little rest too!"

"You . . . you won't leave, will you, Uncle Templeton?" asked Katie.

"No, Kathleen," he said with a smile that seemed a little sad. "I've done too much leaving in my life. For the first time I suppose I care about something other than myself."

Strange to say, his voice was almost quivering as he spoke. I glanced toward him. He was looking straight at me. His eyes met mine and I glanced away.

"No, Kathleen," he added, "I won't leave . . . at least not until I do what I came to do."

Whether she understood what he meant any better than I did, I don't know. But for the moment it seemed to comfort her that he'd said *us* about nobody taking Rosewood away today, and made her feel like she wasn't alone anymore.

"Thank you, Uncle Templeton" was all Katie said. "Thank you for coming back."

I helped Katie to her feet and took her upstairs. She was too exhausted, mentally and physically, for a bath. So I just washed her face and hands and arms and got her into a clean nightgown. Within ten minutes she was sound asleep.

When I went back downstairs to the kitchen, Mr. Daniels was gone.

A Conversation I'd Never Forget

21

THE MORNING PASSED QUIETLY. KATIE SLEPT A long time, and Mr. Daniels busied himself with his horse and then brought his things in and put them in the same room he'd slept in before.

He was quieter than usual, and more somber and kept to himself, which I wouldn't have expected from him. Before when he visited he always had something to say, always with a smile on his lips. Every once in a while I'd see him looking at me from off in the distance, and whenever we happened to pass each other, I kept having the feeling he wanted to say something but couldn't bring himself to it. He looked at me sometimes, and, strange as it is to say it, I thought that he was looking at me as if . . . well, as if he *cared* about me. No white man had ever looked at me like that before. It was the most remarkable thing. It unnerved me. Why would he care about a friend of Katie's that much?

He was different from last time, that much was plain. I wondered if it had something to do with what he'd said to Katie in the kitchen. I didn't know what to make of it, but I went about my business as usual, though it was unsettling to have somebody else around who was acting so strange.

I suppose down inside I was a little bit irritated at him. It wasn't that I wanted him to stay at Rosewood forever or take Katie away with him or anything like that. In fact, it had almost been a relief before when he'd left. But at the same time, I knew Katie was in a fix and he didn't seem to care about doing anything to help. Anyone who wore fancy clothes like he did and talked about winning at poker must have more money than Katie did, and if he was her kin, how could he just leave? I guess I figured that, whatever he'd meant by what he said earlier, I wasn't sure I trusted him not to just up and leave again and not care what happened to Katie.

I didn't exactly know what I felt toward him, which made me confused and frustrated and all the more irritated at him. It made no sense—I'd be the first to admit that. But sometimes feelings don't make sense. Feelings can just sweep over you for no good reason at all. So I reckon the strange way he'd been acting, and not knowing whether he was going to help Katie or not, had kind of gotten under my skin and made me agitated.

And I didn't know why he kept looking at me so funny. It made me uncomfortable. It was just like the time before when he'd stood looking at me upstairs in my room just before he left. Why did he keep looking at me with that strange expression like he wanted to say something?

Sometime a little before noon, I was outside hanging

some wash on the line. Katie was still asleep. She must have been really worn out! I heard a sound behind me.

I turned and there stood Mr. Daniels only three or four feet away. Again he was staring straight into my eyes.

"Hello, Mary Ann," he said. "I'm sorry . . . I didn't mean to startle you."

"How did you know my name?" I said, trying to hide that he *had* startled me and that I'd nearly jumped out of my skin to see him standing there so close!

"I asked Emma," he said with a smile. "She told me."

"Nobody calls me that," I said, going on with the laundry. "Nobody except Katie when she's funning me."

"It's a nice name," he said. "A pretty name."

"Thank you," I said.

"I mean it," he said.

"It ain't like a white man to think kindly about coloreds," I said. I don't know why I said it. It was probably a stupid thing to say to a man I hardly knew, though it was true enough. But once I'd said it I couldn't get it back.

Mr. Daniels chuckled lightly. "You're right about that," he said. "But I've always been a little different than other white men in that regard."

"Why's that?" I asked, starting to relax a little as we talked.

"I reckon because that's how my mama taught me—that's Kathleen's grandmother, her mama's mother. Eliza Jane Daniels, that was her name. She taught Rosalind and Ward and Nelda and me that everyone was equal in God's sight, and that if God had seen fit to make people with different-colored skin, then the least we could do was treat everyone equal."

"Lots of white men go to church but are as mean as can be to coloreds."

"I reckon that's so," he said. "But our mama taught us different. With her it was a real-life way to act, not just some religious words to talk about but ignore when the church doors close. I haven't lived a life I'm completely proud of. But there's one thing I have done that lots of men don't. All my life, when I look at a man or woman, I don't see what color they are. I suppose that's my mama's eyes looking out from mine."

"That's a little like something Henry said once," I said. I finally set down the pins in my hand and stopped trying to hang laundry and talk at the same time.

"Henry?"

"He's the black man who works at the livery stable in town. He found out what we're doing here—how we're all alone. So he's been helping us a lot."

"That's good of him. I'd like to meet him and express my gratitude. So . . . what did he say?"

"He said that the color of a person's skin ain't the color of their heart, and that it's the color of their heart that matters most."

"Then your Henry must be a wise man," smiled Mr. Daniels.

"I don't think he can even read or write," I said.

"That doesn't matter if a man has wisdom," he said. "And what he said about the color of a person's heart is true all right. My mother couldn't have said it better."

It was quiet a minute. Mr. Daniels shuffled about on his feet. I was about to hang another sheet up on the line when he spoke up again.

"Were you . . . uh, born here at Rosewood?" he asked.

"No," I answered.

"You weren't?" He sounded surprised.

"No—don't you remember," I said, "when Katie was telling you what happened when you were here before . . . I didn't come until after the massacre, after both our families were killed. We'd never seen each other before then."

"Oh . . . oh yes, of course. How old are you?"

"Sixteen."

"When is your birthday?"

"I'll be seventeen in August."

He took in what I'd said with a thoughtful look.

"Where were you born, then?" he asked after a few seconds.

I hesitated. Suddenly reminders of William McSimmons flashed through my brain, and I remembered that he was probably still trying to find where Emma was and where I'd disappeared to after they'd tried to hang me. Why was Mr. Daniels asking so many questions? I didn't want to talk about the McSimmons place.

"Uh, on a plantation on the other side of town," I said after a moment.

"Yes . . . that's right. I remember now Katie telling me that before." But he still seemed puzzled. He looked away, and then back at me. His expression was full of question and uncertainty, like he was confused because of what I'd said.

"Mary Ann," he said, "would you mind if I . . . if I ask you a question that's a little personal?"

"I reckon not," I said. I didn't know what kind of a question that was. He'd been asking me questions the whole time we'd been talking. So what was the harm in one more?

"Would you mind telling me . . . what was your mother's name?"

His words were so unexpected that I just stood there staring back at him. What could he possibly care about that?

"I don't know why—" I began.

"Please, I know you may not understand," he said, and his voice sounded almost urgent, "but it is important to me."

"All right, then, I don't reckon there'd be any harm in it," I said. "Her name was Lemuela . . . Lemuela Jukes."

The instant I said the name, his face showed a momentary look of shock, like I'd slapped him across the mouth. He took a step back, still staring at me with an expression stranger than all the rest. His mouth seemed to go dry and his face was pale.

"And . . . and she was killed along with everyone else?" he said, his voice low and husky-like.

"Yes, sir," I said, suddenly feeling very strange.

Mr. Daniels said nothing more. He just turned and walked slowly away.

I didn't see him again for a couple of hours.

THE SHOCK OF MY LIFE

22

I WAS PRETTY BEWILDERED ABOUT HOW THE CONversation with Katie's uncle had ended. And that look on his face was one I'll never forget, though for the life of me I couldn't figure out what it meant. It spooked me. I couldn't get rid of the feeling it left me with. My skin kept crawling every time I thought of it.

I finished the laundry, did a few other chores, and went inside. It was about noon. I fixed Aleta and Emma some lunch, though I wasn't hungry myself and Katie was still asleep. I was feeling too strange to eat. I was cleaning up the lunch things an hour or so later. I heard the outside door open. The others were all upstairs, so I knew it was him.

I heard his footsteps come into the kitchen. Something made me afraid to turn to face him. I felt all jittery. I could feel him standing there looking at me and waiting. Then I heard a chair slide back, and he sat down at the table.

Finally I turned and just stood there with the dish towel in my hands.

"I'm sorry for walking away before," he said.

I kind of nodded, but there wasn't anything to say.

"I know it might be hard for you to understand, but . . . what you said was a shock to me, though I had expected it."

"What . . . you mean about—"

"Yes . . . about your mother," said Mr. Daniels.

"Why was it a shock?" I asked. "What do you mean, you were expecting it? Expecting what?"

"When you told me her name," he answered. "That's what I was expecting. I guess that's what I came back to find out. That's why I had to ask. Although down inside I knew even before I asked. One look at you, once I saw the resemblance, and I knew."

I didn't have any idea what he was talking about.

He paused, and a strange, sad, though happy at the same time, kind of smile came over his face. "You look so much like her," he said. "Especially your eyes, your lips, your forehead. Everything about you reminds me of her. You're a very pretty young lady."

"I don't . . . but . . ." I began, though I didn't even know what I was trying to say. "How could you . . . I mean, what—"

"Mary Ann," he said, "I knew your mother."

I could hardly take it in. I just stared back at him dumbfounded.

"I . . . I don't . . . do you know the McSimmons . . . what did you have to do with . . . I never saw you around the plantation."

"No . . . no, I've never met any of the McSimmons. In fact, I've never heard the name until just now. Is that where you and your family were slaves?"

"Yes, sir."

"And it's near here?"

"Not too far," I said. "I don't know—five or six miles, I reckon."

"I see," he nodded. "No, I've never been there."

"So why did you know my mama?"

"I knew her before she was at the McSimmons'."

That surprised me. I never knew she'd ever lived anywhere else, though I'd never thought much about it.

"Back then, Mary Ann," he added, "believe it or not, your mama lived here at Rosewood."

My eyes shot wide open. Now it was my turn to be shocked.

"But . . . how? Why was she *here*?" I said, finding a chair and sitting down.

"She was Rosalind's house slave," he answered.

"You mean . . . Katie's mama?"

He nodded. "She was never actually a slave—she was Rosalind's friend," he said. "They were raised together up north."

"My mama came from the North?"

"She did. They learned to sew together, to read together, to make pretty things. I was Rosalind's older brother, you see, and I watched them grow up together. Your grandmother, Lemuela's mother, was alone and poor, and let Lemuela live with our family to be Rosalind's maid. They became such good friends, like you and Katie, that when Rosalind married Richard, Lemuela came down here with her as her housemaid."

As I listened I glanced up. There was Katie standing in

the doorway to the parlor. I hadn't even heard her come down the stairs. She was listening intently.

"After Rosalind's marriage," Mr. Daniels went on, "I didn't see either of them for a long time. After a while I wound up down here at Rosewood with Rosalind. Her husband and I never hit it off too well, but since I was kin, he put up with me and let me stay. But the biggest surprise of all was seeing your mama again, now all grown-up. That was in '48."

He paused and his voice got different, like he was thinking back and remembering a long time ago.

"I couldn't keep my eyes off her," he said with a sad smile. "When her work was done, she and I went for long walks—right out there," he said, pointing through the window. "We went walking in those woods almost every evening that autumn as the weather began to turn. It was the happiest time of my life."

He looked at me again, real deep into my eyes like he was staring straight into my soul.

"I grew to love your mother, Mary Ann," he said, ". . . and she loved me too. She was the only woman I ever loved."

His words were confusing and uncomfortable. I was feeling strange and hot, thoughts swirling inside my head. "But . . . but I don't understand," I tried to say, ". . . why was she a *McSimmons* slave if she was here?"

"Because Richard sold her."

"Why did he do that? Why would he sell her if she was Katie's mama's friend?"

Mr. Daniels looked away and I saw him swallow hard,

like he had a lump in his throat. When he spoke again his voice was soft and shaky.

"He sold her . . . because she was carrying my baby."

The room was deathly quiet for several seconds. Katie walked over and took my hand as she sat down beside me. I looked at her, then back at her uncle. My mouth was hanging open.

"Richard hit the roof," he said. "He was so angry that he ran me off and told me never to show my face at Rosewood again. I'm still not sure how he found out because I was never absolutely sure myself. She may have told Rosalind. In any case, before she could tell me, he ran me off, then sold Lemuela, probably through some third party, I don't know. Richard Clairborne was a hard man, but he was as upright and moral as they come. I suppose he didn't want anyone suspecting *him* of what had happened. And he didn't want Lemuela traceable to Rosewood. Even Rosalind never knew where she'd gone. I don't think she ever quite forgave Richard for that. And though I never knew what had happened to her until today, I assumed that she had married and raised a family as a slave on some other plantation."

As I listened, I felt my brain starting to clear, like a pond that you'd thrown rocks in and then it gradually calms until the water stills again so you can see down to the bottom.

"Does that mean . . ." I said, and I could feel Katie's hand squeezing mine "—who . . . who was . . . the baby?"

"Mary Ann," he said, "that's what I have been trying to tell you. The moment you told me how old you were and when you were born, that's when I knew. Mary Ann . . . I am your father."

The room got even quieter than before. The word *father* just hung there in the silence, like it had exploded into my ears. I didn't know what to think . . . what to say . . . what to feel.

I'd hardly known the man I always called my father, the man called Henry Jukes. He was always away working with the men, and I only saw him at night and didn't even remember a time he and I'd had a conversation alone together. Then he died when I was twelve and ever since I'd been used to life without a father at all.

Now suddenly this! A *white man* had just told me he was my father!

Was I really half white? It filled me with such a turmoil of confusion. I suddenly wondered if my name was even Mary Ann Jukes.

Who was I? Had I never been who I thought I was?

Half white! How could such a thing be true?

In the few seconds that we all sat there in silence, such confusion about so many things filled me that gradually I began to get mad. There was no reason for it, but it just happened. And I took it out on Mr. Daniels.

"You mean you were just like William McSimmons," I said, "and my mama was like Emma? You mean . . . you mean—" I sputtered.

It didn't occur to me that I was yelling so loud that Emma was sure to hear. I wasn't thinking very clearly about much of anything right then.

Suddenly I stood up, knocking my chair over, "You mean I'm just . . . just like little William . . . that my daddy wasn't my daddy at all! You did that to my mama!"

My words jolted him. It was the last thing he had

expected. But right then I couldn't see the pain I was causing him, or that my words were like plunging a knife into his heart. I was too bound up in my own emotions to think about anything other than what I was feeling. That's something about young people—they don't pay much attention to how they can hurt grown-ups, especially their parents, by what they say and do. All they can think about is themselves, and that's what I was doing right then. I would regret it later, but I couldn't see it then.

I flew around the table and began hitting him. I was so angry. But he just sat there and let me pound on him until I stopped yelling and started to cry and stepped back. As I did I glanced across the room.

There were Emma and Aleta standing in the doorway. All the yelling had brought them downstairs to see what was going on. I saw William in Emma's arms and thought of my poor mama and what disgrace and grief she must have felt. I knew I'd been born a slave, but hadn't figured on being a bastard slave. I couldn't help it—my anger came back to the surface again. I turned back to Katie's uncle.

"How could you have left her!" I cried.

"If I had just known . . ." he began.

"You would probably still have left," I shot back, "because you're nothing but a coward."

It was a cruel thing to say. He sat silent as a stone.

"You made my mother into . . . into—"

I couldn't even say it but ran out of the house.

Anger, Tears, and Silence
23

When I got outside, I ran and ran until eventually I found myself at Katie's quiet place in the woods.

Angrily I picked up some small stones and threw them as hard as I could into the stream. Finally I began to tire and crumpled crying onto the ground.

I probably dozed off. Crying does that to you. Gradually I felt something wet on my cheek. It startled me awake. Rusty was licking at the tears that had dried on my face. As I opened my eyes I saw Katie standing behind him.

She sat down on the ground beside me and put her arm around my neck. Neither of us said anything. I felt ashamed. Seeing Katie made me start crying again. She waited while I babbled and cried. I was still pretty mixed up, feeling both guilty and stupid, yet still I couldn't get past the anger I felt at Mr. Daniels for what he'd done to my mother.

Finally Katie spoke. Her voice was calm and steady, and it was the first time she'd ever done anything like this before.

It just showed what a friend she was that she loved me enough to tenderly tell me I was wrong.

"You really hurt Uncle Templeton by what you said, Mayme," she said. "I think you wronged him."

I sniffled and halfway nodded. I knew it was true. I was feeling bad enough about it already.

"He was trying to reach out to you, Mayme," said Katie softly. "I think you owe him an apology."

"But what about what he did?" I said, getting defensive.

"What did he do, Mayme—fall in love with your mother? Are you going to hold that against him? Just think about what I'm saying instead of arguing. Think how you'd feel if he had gotten angry at you."

"It's different," I said.

"Maybe it is. But he can't go back and undo it, Mayme. So he's trying to make it right now. Maybe it's taken him a long time, but what else can he do? He didn't know."

I sat in silence trying to sort through it all.

"Besides, Mayme," Katie went on, "if what he said is true, that he's your father, then he gave you life and helped make you what you are. How can you be mad at him for that? If he had never known your mama, you'd never have been born."

Right now I was too confused with so many feelings that it was hard to get my brain to make sense of that. The thought of being half white and half colored had spun my mind around so bad it made me feel like I wasn't even a real person at all.

"What do you want me to do, Katie?" I said finally. "I can't think straight. Just tell me what I ought to do."

"Don't you think you ought to talk to him?" she said. "He is your father."

There was that word again. It felt both warm and hateful at the same time. How could the word *father* arouse so many conflicting emotions in a young person's heart?

I wiped my eyes and nose, splashed some cold water from the stream on my face, then stood up and tried to smile.

"All right," I said. "I'll try."

Katie and I walked back to the house. Emma was in the kitchen. She glanced up and I saw from her face that I'd hurt her too. I could see that she was both mad at me and hurt by the things I'd said about her and William.

"He's in da barn," she said coldly, then went upstairs without even looking in my direction.

Katie looked at me, and I knew what I had to do.

Slowly I walked outside and across the yard to the barn. It was about the longest that walk had ever seemed in my life. There's no way to describe what I was feeling. I didn't even know myself. My heart was pounding so loud it seemed like I could almost hear it.

I opened the door. It creaked and light poured into the barn. There he was standing on the other side with his horse. He had just thrown a saddle up on its back.

He turned to face me. Again our eyes met. Everything had now changed. The look on his face was different. I saw the pain. And I knew I had caused it.

"I'm sorry for what you think, Mayme," he said. "I suppose you're right about my being a selfish man. I've always been selfish. I don't deny it. And maybe I was a coward too, like you said. Maybe your words bit so deep because they're true. But I loved your mama, that much is true. And when I told you that she was the only woman I ever loved, that's God's truth. There was never anyone else."

My eyes were stinging with tears.

"I don't know what happened with Emma," he went on, "but it wasn't like what you think. I don't know if you can understand. I'd like to think you can. But there's no way for a white man to love a black woman in this country. But we loved each other. I even offered to buy her from Katie's father, but he wouldn't hear of it. After he ran me off, that was just about when the gold rush was breaking. I went out west with Ward. Maybe I shouldn't have, but it was my way of trying to forget. He went to hunt for gold, but I didn't want to work that hard. I discovered gambling in San Francisco and found I was pretty good at it. While Ward stayed on in California I returned east on a ship, gambling my way all the way around South America. But then I really didn't have anyplace to call home. And I *couldn't* forget. All I could think of was your mother, so I came back to look for her. I never knew for sure whether there had been a child. I always wondered. Rosalind didn't know where she was and I could never find out. And if she couldn't forgive Richard, I don't think she ever forgave me either for taking away her friend. After that I began drifting and have been drifting ever since, but I could never make anything of myself. I reckon I never will. But I always wanted to find her. I never knew until I saw you upstairs a few months ago. Suddenly I saw Lemuela's eyes staring back at me."

"Then why did you leave?" I asked.

"I don't know. I suppose I was afraid . . . afraid of what it might mean. I just couldn't cope with the idea of having . . . having a child . . . one that I had never known. I don't know why. Seems like I've always been running from something. But that's why I came back. I'd never been able to find out where your mama was. And ever since I saw that look in your eyes, I haven't been able to sleep nights, wondering . . . hoping that maybe she was still alive. And now I find out that you . . . and that she's . . ."

His voice faltered and he looked away.

When you're young you have no idea how hard it is for a grown-up, especially a man, to open himself up and let people look at what he's feeling inside. I reckon that's what folks call being vulnerable. It's hard to be vulnerable, but it's a gift some people have and it makes them better people. But right then I still had eyes only for myself and I couldn't realize what it meant that he was opening up such a window into himself and allowing me, his own daughter, to look into it. I had no idea how hard that was for him, or what a special thing it is for a daughter to be able to look into her father's heart.

He stared down at the ground for a second, then back up at me. He didn't know what more to say. I didn't either.

We just stood there—a white man and a colored sixteen-year-old girl—neither of us knowing how to bridge the gap between us. The man who had always considered himself footloose and fancy-free had just discovered he had a daughter . . . and a black one at that. The girl who always thought of herself as the black daughter of Henry Jukes had just discovered that her father was alive after all, and was somebody else . . . and that he was white!

After a minute he turned and went back to saddling his horse.

"What . . . are you doing?" I asked.

"I reckon it's time I was moving on again," he said without turning around.

"Why?"

"This isn't my home," he said. "I don't know what I was expecting. Maybe it never could be . . . not now . . . not after this. You're not looking for a father, at least not one who's white, and maybe I was just fooling myself in thinking I was looking for a family. She's dead and you got your own life now. It's probably best we forget this whole thing."

I just stood there like a statue, hot tears stinging my eyes.

He finished with the saddle and led his horse outside through the big door. I turned and took a few steps outside and then stood watching him. He led his horse across the yard, dropped the reins, and went into the house. I knew he was saying good-bye to Katie. A minute or two later he came back outside, Katie following him. Her eyes were red. She glanced over at me where I stood by the barn.

Mr. Daniels climbed up into the saddle, then reined his horse around and walked him slowly in my direction. He stopped and looked down at me where I stood.

"Good-bye, Mayme," he said.

"Good . . . good-bye," I said, though my voice was barely a whisper.

This time he didn't look into my eyes. Instead he glanced away, then eased his horse around and toward the road.

I watched him go, my heart exploding in agony inside me, but unable to utter a sound.

Clomp . . . clomp . . . clomp . . . went the hooves of his horse as he slowly disappeared up the road toward the

Thurston ranch in the opposite direction from Greens Crossing.

When he was almost to the bend into the woods I heard the kitchen door close. I looked toward the house. Katie had gone inside. I turned back and peered down the road.

Katie's uncle had disappeared from sight.

I stood and stared after him another minute or two more and then went back into the barn. I found a dark corner where I could lie down on some straw. I burst into tears and wept more bitterly than I had even after my family was killed, and finally cried myself to sleep.

Looking Inside
24

THINGS WERE DIFFERENT AFTER THAT.

Emma was mad at me and hardly spoke a word for days. And she had every right to be mad. I'd said terrible things about her and William, but right then the words *I'm sorry* were too hard for me to say. They ought to be such easy words for people to say to each other, but for some reason they're not. People seem to choke on the two words that would make the world such a kindlier and happier place. And with Emma hardly talking and keeping to herself, Rosewood was quieter than I ever remembered it since the first day I'd come.

Whether Katie was mad at me or not, I couldn't tell. But things were different, that was for sure. She was polite, but we didn't talk anymore. It grew silent and distant between us. My heart ached because of it. Every once in a while I heard Katie and Emma talking in another room and they were talking like Katie and I used to. I found myself thinking that Emma was now going to become Katie's best friend. I wasn't jealous. I was just sad for what I'd lost. Everything about Rosewood had changed, and somehow I knew it was my fault.

The days passed like a sad dream. Now it was my turn to go on long, thoughtful walks by myself. I visited Katie's secret place in the woods a few times, sometimes just to be alone and cry, other times to think and try to figure out who I was. Just when I'd begun to think I had it figured out and when I'd gotten used to the idea of being free and being all alone in the world, I had a lot that was new to get used to.

It felt like love and anger and confusion were all at war inside me. Maybe it was my white side and my black side fighting against each other. If blacks and whites fought between themselves, then imagine what it was like for that fight to be going on inside one person!

As hard as my life had been, as hard as being a slave was, I'd been at peace with it in a way, even proud in a way for the heritage that the color of my skin gave me, proud of my people, proud of their culture even if they had been slaves. I don't exactly know what words to put to the feeling. I reckon it's something only a black person could understand. It's a hard thing being colored. But there was never a moment in my life when I'd have traded it for anything else. I never wanted to be white. It's hard, but still there's a pride a black person feels in who they are.

Suddenly that feeling was turned upside down. Half of me carried the blood of the white masters, the blood of those who had whipped me and hung black men to die and raped their women.

Things gradually came back into my memory too—

unpleasant things I'd forced myself to forget. I was just a child, but I remembered the talk, the looks, the stares, being made fun of by other kids because of my lighter skin. . . . *Look at her, she's half white.* I recalled things that had happened through my childhood and talk around the slave village, and things I'd heard Josepha say. The talk had hurt at the time, but I'd blocked it out of my mind so thoroughly that only now it began to come back to me. It was no different than the way I'd been toward William at first.

I remembered too that other slaves always treated Mama different and seemed to resent that she could do more than them, that she was more polished, more refined, that she could read. Everything Mr. Daniels had told me fit with what I remembered. I knew he was telling the truth. It made it all make sense. Yet it made me hate him for what he'd put me and my mama through.

I couldn't resolve it. It was almost like now I had someone to blame for my hard life, for my being a slave, and for the massacre that had killed my family, for the wrong he had done to my mother both by getting her pregnant and abandoning her. It felt good to hate him. Yet it didn't really feel good because it was eating me up inside. How could I hate him without hating myself at the same time?

One day I was standing in front of a mirror. I began noticing things about my face and nose and hair and cheeks and eyes that I hadn't paid much attention to before. I *wasn't* as dark as Emma. My skin was a lighter brown, and when I smiled, there was just a hint of Templeton Daniels' smile staring back at me. There was no denying it.

It's hard to put into words what it's like for a black person to find out they're half white. There's just about no shock like it. I suppose it might be the same for anybody learning something about themselves they never knew before, except that black blood isn't so easy to hide as white. Everyone knows if you've got black blood in you. But I'd never known that I had white blood in me.

Suddenly I didn't know who I was anymore. Was I white or was I black . . . or half and half? If so, what did that mean? To realize that I was just like William made me realize that there'd been more ill feelings of prejudice in my heart than I realized.

Maybe none of us knows ourselves as well as we think we do. I guess I'd grown pretty satisfied with who I was, and I reckon that's a mighty dangerous thing to be. Once you're satisfied with who you are, that's when you stop growing inside. Now that I looked down inside I saw some ugly things. I reckon it's our own hearts whose foul colors we're most blind to. I sure wouldn't have wanted anyone to see my heart right then!

The fact that God saw it, and knew what was in it well enough, was none too comforting a thought!

One day I came upon Emma alone in the kitchen fixing William some warm milk.

"Do you mind if I hold him?" I asked.

Emma shot a few daggers at me with her eyes, then said, "No, I reckon not."

I stooped down and picked William off the floor where he was crawling about. "You want to come outside with me for a minute, William?" I said. He just babbled some unintelligible sounds at me and tried to grab my nose with his fat little fingers.

I left the kitchen and walked outside holding him close

to me. He was such a pleasant, happy baby. His black hair was as kinky as Emma's, but his skin was obviously lighter, there was no doubt about that. Yes, he was half white and his father was a scoundrel besides. But William was still William and we all loved him, Emma most of all. He was still a little child of God, whoever else's child he might be too.

Then Henry's words came back to me, and they stung me right to my heart for the bad things I'd thought and said.

No, William, I whispered into his ear as I held his little head close to mine, *the color of your skin, or your daddy's, ain't the color of your heart, is it? And I reckon if that's true for you, it oughta be true for me too. You and me may be half white, but we're both God's children, ain't we? So maybe we gotta learn to be who God wants us to be, even if we're a little different from everybody else.*

I guess you'd say from that moment on, the dark cloud began to lift off my soul. Sometimes it takes realizing something with your brain to snap your heart back where it oughta be. My heart hadn't been where it should have been for a while, but I hoped now maybe it could start getting some of its right color back.

I went back inside. Emma was still in the kitchen. I set William down on the floor and walked over to her. It was hard to get her to face me because she was still looking away with an angry look on her face.

"Emma . . ." I said, "Emma . . . please look at me."

Slowly she turned.

"Emma, I am so sorry," I said. "I was wrong to say what I said. I love you. Can you ever forgive me?"

Emma's eyes filled with tears and the scowl melted from

her face. She threw her arms around me, crying like a baby.

"Oh, dat I can, Mayme . . . dat I can. You been so good ter me, I couldn't stay mad at you. I jes' thought you din't like me or William no mo."

"That wasn't it, Emma," I said. "I was just mixed up about myself, that's all. I'm so sorry I took it out on you."

"Dat all right, Mayme. It be all ober now, an' I ain't gwine think no mo 'bout it."

"Thank you, Emma," I said, stepping back and smiling. "I reckon there's somebody else I need to say I'm sorry to, too."

"If you be meanin' Miz Katie," said Emma, "her heart's full er forgiveness, I kin say dat, 'cuz I know. She been hurtin' fer you, but she ain't been mad like me."

"I know, Emma. But I've still got to say it."

I left the kitchen and found Katie upstairs. She looked up as I walked in. She knew immediately there had been a change. She stood up and walked straight to me and we fell into each other's arms.

We stood there for the longest time, holding each other and crying.

"I'm sorry, Katie," I said finally. "I'm so sorry. I don't know what got into me."

"It's over now, Mayme," she whispered. "That's all that matters."

Somehow all that had happened and all the turmoil and grief that had gotten mixed up between us that had turned Rosewood into such a quiet, somber place for a few days had kept us from seeing the thing that would change our lives. Probably most of you saw it a long time ago, but I was so mixed up I didn't see it, and Katie was so sad she didn't see it either.

But once we'd hugged each other and I'd said I was sorry, the sun came back out. Suddenly the light dawned on us of what it meant that Templeton Daniels was my father. Actually, it dawned on Katie first.

It was only about an hour after I'd gone up to her room when suddenly I heard Katie shrieking and yelling.

I thought something was horribly wrong or that she'd been hurt. I dashed back toward the house from the barn where I'd just gone to begin the evening milking.

Katie came running out of the house, her face aglow and her eyes wide, running toward me and waving her arms.

"Mayme . . . Mayme!" she cried, laughing like she could hardly contain herself, then hugging me and dancing around. I'd never seen her with such a huge smile on her face.

"What is it?" I asked, realizing there was no danger and unable to keep from laughing too, though I didn't know what we were laughing about.

"Don't you see!" exclaimed Katie. "Mayme . . . we're cousins!"

The word hit me harder than the word *father* had earlier.

"We've got the same grandmother. Your papa is my uncle. My mama is your aunt. Mayme . . . we're kin . . . we're actually cousins! We are family. Our families *aren't* all dead. We have each other. You have a papa and I have an uncle. We have a family!"

If being half white meant I got to be Katie's cousin, then all of a sudden it seemed about the greatest thing in the world that could have happened to me!

Emma and Aleta

25

FROM THAT DAY ON THINGS BEGAN TO BRIGHTEN and gradually we started to get back to normal. But what was normal now, with me knowing I was Templeton Daniels' daughter and Katie's cousin!

And the question that loomed in the midst of it all was whether I would ever see him again.

Neither Katie nor me realized how much Mr. Daniels' disclosure worked on Emma and Aleta too. I suppose the two of us tended to think about what we were thinking and what to do about ourselves, and just figured it would be best for all of us. But that's not always so. Sometimes it's easy to overlook other people's thoughts and feelings. We didn't realize how much Aleta and Emma were thinking about things too. Even Emma wasn't altogether the lamebrain folks took her for, or that I had taken her for at first either. She'd been paying attention. She knew she was free now just as well as I did. And down inside she was thinking about what it meant, and what the future might hold for her.

I hardly noticed that she was a little quieter than usual right after that. Like I said, I was too involved thinking about myself to see how this change might affect her. Katie and I were so happy to find out we were cousins, we could hardly think about anything else. We just figured everybody'd be happy along with us.

And they were, of course. But things like that don't affect everyone the same way. And we had no idea how Emma was reacting inside to the change, or that there was actually a part of it that made her thoughtful and even a little sad.

She wandered into one of the bedrooms one afternoon when William was napping. Aleta was standing at the window with her back turned.

"What you lookin' at, Miz Aleta?" said Emma.

"Nothing," said Aleta. "Just Katie and Mayme out there at the washtub."

Emma walked over and stood beside her. They stood there staring out at us for a minute. We were laughing and talking and happy—that much was obvious to anybody looking at us for a second. It was just three days after it had dawned on us that we were kin, and we were about as full of joy as any two girls could possibly be. What we'd found out had completely changed everything about our lives.

"Dey's mighty happy 'bout it," said Emma after a minute.

Aleta nodded.

"It's right fine fer Miz Mayme, ain't it, dat she's got a daddy after all?"

"I wish I had a nice daddy like that," said Aleta.

"I wish I had me a daddy at all," said Emma, "leastways one dat I knew who he wuz. But I ain't."

They stood watching us for a while without saying anything.

"Dey got each other," said Emma after a bit. "Dey got each other an' dey got Mr. Daniels."

"He's gone," said Aleta.

"I reckon dat's so. But dey know dey got kinfolk—dat counts fer somefin', don't it? I ain't got nobody like dat, Miz Aleta. I ain't got nobody ter call kinfolk in da whole worl' 'cept my William."

Again it was quiet. Aleta was only ten. How much she understood of what was going on inside Emma's heart right then was hard to say. Emma was a mother too, and becoming a parent grows a person up mighty quick—that is, if they've got the humility to see what it means.

"What's gwine happen t' us, Miz Aleta, do you suppose?" said Emma. "You reckon dis'll change things?"

"I don't know," said Aleta, still staring down into the yard.

"Whatever happens, ain't nothin' gwine happen dat dey can't git through. An' effen dere was, Mr. Daniels, he'd take care ob dem now, 'cause he's kin. But you don't figger he'd do dat fer us, do you? We ain't no kin. Who we got, Miz Aleta? We ain't got nobody. You got yer daddy, I reckon, but I ain't got nobody what cares fer me like dat, no frien' like dey is t' each other. William's daddy, he'd like ter kill me. An' now dere ain't no tellin' what's gwine happen. Dat Mr. Daniels, he's a nice enuff man, but he might come an' take Rosewood, or maybe take Miz Katie an' Miz Mayme away t' wherever he lives. Dat's what kinfolk does. An' den what's t' become ob us. It's all boun' ter change now, Miz Aleta, an' I ain't got nobody like dat, an' what's gwine happen t' me an' my William effen he does? He ain't gwine want no dumb nigger like me roun'."

"You're not dumb, Emma," said Aleta.

"You's right kind, Miz Aleta."

"I wish you wouldn't use that word you said about yourself," Aleta added. "It reminds me of how my daddy talks. I don't like to hear it anymore."

"But you know I ain't smart like Miz Mayme an' Miz Katie."

"You know how to take care of William," said Aleta. "You're about the best mother I've ever seen, Emma, except for mine."

"You's so kind, Miz Aleta! Dat's 'bout da bes' thing anybody's eber said ter me!"

This time they stared out the window watching for a longer time without saying anything. At last Aleta spoke up.

"I'll take care of you, Emma," she said. "I'll be your friend."

"Dat's right kind ob you, Miz Aleta," said Emma. "Yes, sir—dat's right kind. But you's jes' a little girl. How old you be, Miz Aleta?"

"Ten."

"Dat's a fine age, all right. But I'm sebenteen—leastways, I think I'm sebenteen, but I ain't too good wiff figgerin' numbers an' like dat. An' I don't reckon a ten-year-old can take care ob no seventeen-year-old what's got a baby. Right now, Miz Katie an' Miz Mayme, dey been takin' care ob us and givin' us food an' dis place ob deres t' stay. I reckon we'd jes' 'bout be dead effen dey hadn't been takin' care ob us. Wiffout dem, I don't reckon I'd know what ter do."

"But if we stay together, Emma," said Aleta, at last turning to face her, "if we're friends like Katie and Mayme, we could help take care of each other. You could help take care of me too."

Emma turned to face her and looked down at her with a smile. Emma was so tall and thin, she must have stood a foot higher than Aleta.

"I reckon dat's so, Miz Aleta!" she said. "Yes, sir, I reckon you's right at dat!"

"Maybe we'll find out that we're cousins too, Emma!" said Aleta excitedly.

"I don't rightly think dat could be," said Emma.

"Why not?"

" 'Cause look at my skin. I'm as black as an ol' coon."

"Katie and Mayme don't look like each other either. Katie's white and Mayme's black."

"She ain't altogether black. One look at Miz Mayme an' you can see dat dere's white blood mixed in dere. Don' you see da difference, Miz Aleta?"

"I never thought about it."

"Well, one look at me an' you can see dat dere ain't a drop ob white blood in me nohow."

"That doesn't matter," said Aleta. "If we're friends, we can still take care of each other. My daddy cares what color people are, and I used to care. But I don't anymore."

It got quiet again. Aleta smiled and took Emma's hand, then they both turned back to the window. They stood together, hand in hand, for several more minutes, until they heard William beginning to make noises in the other room.

THE HEAVY LANTERN

26

THOUGH THE SUN HAD COME OUT BETWEEN ME and Katie, there was still one big cloud in the sky of our future that loomed as large as Emma's worries about her own. Katie hadn't forgotten it either.

A few days later I found Katie seated at her mama's desk looking at the letter from the bank.

"Uncle Templeton's visit almost made me forget," she said. "The loan is still due. We may have only three weeks left at Rosewood."

I sat down on the other side of the room.

"If we could only find the gold!" said Katie in frustration.

"Do you really think there's more?" I said. "Your uncle said he didn't think there was."

"I don't know, Mayme! Maybe I just want to believe there is, because if there isn't, then the bank will take Rosewood."

We sat for a few minutes in silence.

"If your uncle had given your mama his gold," I said after a bit, "where do you think she'd hide it?"

"I don't know. In the cellar, I suppose. That's always what I thought. Where else could it possibly be? It's the most hidden part of the whole house."

"Why don't we go down there and look?" I suggested.

"I've looked everywhere!"

"It wouldn't hurt to try again."

A few minutes later we were standing down underneath the floor beams of the parlor again.

"I've looked in all the places I can think of, Mayme," said Katie, glancing about. "I'm just out of ideas."

"What about that furniture over there?" I said.

"I looked in all those drawers and inside the cabinet. I've gone through every box and everything on those shelves. It's all just junk, like those old lanterns. Look at them—they're just old and getting rusty and dirty. There's no sign of anything valuable. My mama and daddy only put junk down here they wanted to get rid of and had no room for anywhere else."

"What about that barrel? What's it for?"

"Just to store a few potatoes in for the winter."

"Maybe it could be inside there," I said. "Maybe they took the potatoes out."

Katie's eyes shot open. The next instant she was across the floor trying to pry the lid off the barrel.

"It's stuck, Mayme," she said. "Come help me!"

But try as we might, we couldn't get the lid off.

"I'll get a hammer," said Katie excitedly. Already she was halfway up the ladder into the house. She was on her way back down in less than two minutes and hurrying across to the barrel.

Two or three whacks from the underside loosened the lid. I managed to get my fingers under one side, then Katie whacked at it again.

"I think it's coming, Katie," I said. "Can you pull up on the other side?"

We both struggled for all we were worth. Suddenly the stuck lid gave way and popped off the barrel and fell to the floor.

"Ugh . . . that stinks!" cried Katie as she jumped back from the barrel. The most foul smell imaginable was coming from inside.

I held my nose and peered inside.

"There's only about a foot of whatever it was left in the bottom," I said. "It's all rotten and squishy and brown."

"I guess there's no gold in there!" said Katie, holding her nose too. "Let's get the lid back on . . . ugh, that's horrible!"

A minute later we had the lid back on, though the smell didn't go away immediately.

"What about underneath it?" I said. "Maybe they dug a hole and rolled the barrel on top of it to hide it."

"Let's look!" said Katie.

Rolling the smelly potato barrel to one side was even harder than getting the lid off. We pushed against the top and tipped it a little to one side and then struggled to roll the bottom of it. But we could only get it to move six or eight inches at a time before the weight of it plopped back down onto the dirt. And we couldn't help being a little timid of it for fear that some of the liquid goo in the bottom was going to splash up and come through the cracks and get on us. It took five or six attempts to get it away from where it had been before. When we did, there wasn't a sign that the dirt had been disturbed.

By then we had so much invested that we didn't want to give up without looking. Katie got the shovel from where it was leaning against the wall from the last time she had been down here. Then we took turns digging up the dirt under where the barrel had been. But after fifteen minutes we realized we weren't going to find anything there either.

"What about under any of this other stuff?" I said.

"I don't know," said Katie, getting frustrated again. "Why would it be there?"

"Because maybe they dug a hole and put all this stuff on top of it to hide it."

"I suppose it's worth a try."

"Let's move some of these things out of the way," I said, "and scoot the furniture back."

I picked up a small wooden crate and carried it across the floor. Katie grabbed at the old lantern that was beside it. She couldn't lift it but dragged it across the floor, where the bottom edge of the metal cut a line through the dirt from its weight.

"Why is this old lantern *so* heavy!" she said, straining to tug it away.

"It's made of brass," I said.

"But brass isn't *that* heavy!"

Finally she got it out of the way. We returned to the corner with the stuff in it when suddenly behind us the lantern we'd brought down flickered and began to go out.

"We'd better turn up the wick," I said.

"No, it's not the wick," said Katie. "It's out of oil. I knew it was low but I forgot to fill it."

"Should I go up and get some more?" I asked.

Just then the lantern went out and we were left in darkness except for what little light came down from the opening up into the parlor.

"I've got some matches right here," said Katie. "I'll try to light this old heavy one."

She took the matches out of the pocket of her dress. But after lighting three or four, she couldn't get the wick to take. She felt it with her fingers.

"It's completely dry," she said. "How can it not have oil when the base is so heavy? I thought it was full of oil.—Here, Mayme," she said, handing me several matches and the striker. "Strike a match and I'll look."

I did, then held the match down toward the large round base of the lantern while Katie knelt and tried to unfasten the lid of the oil chamber.

"It's stuck too," she said. "I can't get it."

The match I was holding burned out. I lit another.

Again Katie struggled with the lid. "I think I managed to loosen it," she said, ". . . here it comes."

As the lid popped off I heard Katie exclaim in astonishment. But just then the match went out.

"What was it, Katie?" I said as I fumbled to light another. "Was there oil in it?"

"I don't think so, Mayme," she said. Her voice was trembling. "Hurry . . . hurry, Mayme! I think there was something else inside the lantern . . . something dry and yellow . . . something that doesn't burn!"

Another match flashed into fire in between my fingers.

Together Katie and I stared down at the base of the lantern whose top she had just removed. The oil chamber was empty of oil, all right. The oil had been taken out and something else hidden there in its place.

"Gold!" we both said at once.

But we hardly had time to look at it for more than a second or two when the match went out again.

"Now I am going to get some more oil!" I said.

I handed the matches and striker back to Katie and ran for the stairs. But as I reached the parlor I realized we didn't want to fill a lantern. We wanted to see what was inside that oil chamber! So I just grabbed one of the parlor lanterns and hurried back down with it into the cellar. In another minute we again had light about us from the new lantern, and Katie and I were seated staring at what we'd discovered.

"I don't believe it," said Katie, shaking her head. "We've been looking for it all this time, and I see it with my own eyes, but I just don't believe it."

"No wonder you couldn't light the lantern!" I said. "Gold is a lot heavier than oil!"

"And here it was all the time, right under our noses . . . in plain view!"

"That must be what your mama figured," I said. "She sure hid it in a place nobody'd think to look for it. We didn't!"

"I guess I will be going to see Mr. Taylor tomorrow!" said Katie, finally starting to laugh. "He will really not believe it! Wow—can you imagine . . . my uncle's gold hidden right in the oil chamber of this old lantern that I thought my mother had just thrown away!"

Mr. Taylor's Eyes Pop Out

27

It seemed like we were always coming and going from the bank and that we were always having to worry about money. And I guess that was true. Money was what made the world work the way it did. And when Katie's mother had taken out those two loans during the war to keep Rosewood going while Katie's father and brothers were gone to fight, it meant that money would be at the root of Rosewood's problems until the loans were either paid off or else the plantation taken away from the Clairborne family altogether.

And so here we were heading to the bank again. But this time we had something with us that we hoped would put the problem with money behind us for good and make it so that Katie didn't ever have to worry about it again.

We pulled up in front of the bank. Katie gave me a look that said, *Well, here goes nothing!*

"I'll wait for you here," I said.

"Oh no," said Katie, climbing down from the wagon.

"You're coming with me, Mayme. We found this together and you're as much a part of Rosewood now as I am, even if my name is *Clairborne* and yours isn't."

"But do you really want—" I began.

"Yes," Katie interrupted with a determined smile. "—I want you with me. If you're still worried about what people think, Mayme, don't you know by now that I don't care? And we've both got half Daniels blood in us, don't forget that. And this is Daniels gold, not Clairborne gold, which I figure makes it half yours."

Sometimes there was no arguing with Katie! I nodded, returning her smile, and got down from the other side of the wagon. Then together we walked toward the door of the bank.

There were two or three other men who worked in the bank and who were used to seeing Katie by now and called her by name as we walked inside. But as we made our way toward the manager's desk, and when Mr. Taylor glanced up and saw us approaching, the expression on his face was one that had an unmistakable hint of annoyance on it. Every time he tried to see or talk to Katie's mother, the only person he could actually talk to was Katie, and he had gotten a mite exasperated by it.

"Hello, Miss Clairborne," he said a little coldly as we stopped in front of his desk. He didn't so much as glance at me. It was as if I wasn't even there. "I assume you are here concerning your mother's loan."

"Yes, sir," said Katie.

"No doubt to tell me that your mother couldn't come herself and sent you instead," he went on, "and that she wants you to tell me that she doesn't have the money quite yet and that she would like to ask me to be patient and extend the due date just a few months."

"No, sir."

"I'm sorry, Miss Clairborne, but as I explained in—"

Suddenly he seemed to realize what Katie had just said.

"That's not why I'm here," said Katie.

"Then . . . what is the purpose of this visit?" asked the bank manager, now more confused than irritated.

"To pay off the loan, Mr. Taylor," said Katie. "Or at least part of it."

She reached into the pocket of her dress and pulled out the handful of nuggets she'd put there. She set them gleaming and yellow on his desk right in front of him.

The man's eyes got big and wide as Katie pulled her hand away and he saw the eight pieces of gold lying there in front of him.

I thought his eyes were going to pop right out of his head! It was deathly quiet for a few seconds. I think the other men in the bank had been sort of secretly watching, and the moment Katie pulled out the chunks of gold, their jaws had dropped too.

Finally Mr. Taylor reached forward and picked up one of the chunks to examine it more closely, and then his voice broke the silence.

"Why . . . why, there must be eight, maybe ten ounces here."

"Yes, sir."

"But where did you get them?"

"Do you remember me telling you about my uncle," answered Katie, "when I brought you those gold coins to put in our account?"

"Yes . . . yes, of course. You said he'd gone to California and had come back with some gold he'd left your mama for safekeeping."

"Yes, sir. Well, he left this with my mama too—besides the coins. He gave it to her to keep for him and take care of."

"Where is your uncle now?"

"We don't know, sir."

"Has your mother had this all along?"

"Yes, sir."

"Then why did she take out the loans?"

"Because she didn't want to use her brother's gold, sir. It wasn't ours and she thought he might come back for it."

"But now she *is* prepared to use it toward the loan?"

"Yes, sir."

"Why is that?"

"Because we think . . . that is, my mother thinks he might *not* come back for it after all. My other uncle thinks he's dead, and so it's not worth losing Rosewood just to wait and find out."

"Yes . . . yes, of course. That makes a great deal of sense. Well, well, Miss Clairborne, this certainly does change things," he said, now almost smiling for the first time.

"Will this be enough to pay off my mama's second loan?" asked Katie.

"Well . . . I am not sure really. Three hundred fifty dollars is a lot of money, and you know, of course, Kathleen, that one cannot simply put pieces of gold like this into a bank account."

"Oh . . ." replied Katie. She sounded surprised.

"It must be weighed," said Mr. Taylor. "You have to

find out what it is worth. That should not be a problem," he added. "—I can take care of it for you. I'll take it to Oakwood. But that will take time. I cannot actually credit your account—that is, your mother's account—until the gold is valued and is sold. Perhaps that is what your mother wanted me to do."

"Yes, sir," nodded Katie. "But how long will it take . . . what about the loan?"

"I will see to it in plenty of time that the deadline does not pass, you can be sure of that."

"Thank you, Mr. Taylor."

"Fine, then—it is all settled," he said. "I will see to the technicalities and advise your mother of the proceeds. Shall I apply the entire sum as payment on the loan?"

"Uh . . . yes, sir—that will be fine. We're hoping . . . that is, my mother hopes with the balance in our account that this will be enough for the loan."

"I should think that might be possible, even likely. Why don't I just consult the ledger and see where we stand."

He stood and went to a cabinet and pulled out a drawer and then took out a file. A minute later he returned.

"Your account presently stands at one hundred eighty-seven dollars," he said. "It was down to one hundred fourteen, and then with your deposit of seventy-three dollars last month, that brought the total up to the one hundred eighty-seven. As I said, the loan is three hundred fifty dollars, so judging from the weight of what you've brought me, I would think it would be sufficient to cover it.—I shall place these in the safe," he added with a smile, scooping up the nuggets in his hand. "We don't want anything to happen to them, do we!"

"No, sir," said Katie, glancing around. It was good there weren't any other customers in the bank right then, especially Mrs. Hammond! We just had to make sure *she* didn't hear about this or the whole world would find out! "And . . . you won't tell anyone about the gold, will you?" Katie added. "Mama wanted me to make sure of that too."

"No, of course not. It will be our secret. I will put these into a sealed envelope before I place them in the safe. Nobody but the bank employees will know."

"I would like to take out ten dollars from the account too, please," said Katie.

"Of course. I will see to that too."

He left for a few minutes. When he returned, his hands were empty except for the ten dollars Katie had asked for.

"Well then, Kathleen," he said, "I shall be in touch with you." Then he smiled. "I must say that this is the most unusual payment I have ever received in all my years of banking. Imagine, a tiny little gold rush right here in Greens Crossing!"

A few minutes later we walked back to the buggy, Katie clutching the first ten-dollar bill I'd ever set eyes on in my life.

She climbed up, turned the horses around in the street, and we headed back toward the general store, where we wanted to buy some things before returning to Rosewood.

"Let me see it!" I said as we rode along.

Katie handed it to me. I was surprised that it just felt like a little piece of paper. A coin made of gold felt like money. And looked valuable too. But how could a piece of paper be worth so much!

Home and New Questions

28

THE NEXT SEVERAL DAYS WERE ABOUT THE HAPpiest ones since Katie and I had been together. I'd never seen Katie in such jubilant spirits.

And I guess I was too. It was happening slow, but it was gradually sinking in just what an almighty wonderful thing had happened between us—that we had learned to love each other, learning to help and care for each other and to live together and fend for ourselves with each other, and then after all that to find out we'd been related all along.

Cousins! I still could hardly believe it!

But like I said, it was slowly sinking in.

And the other thing it was doing was giving me a feeling of *belonging*. That's one of the things about being a slave—you never feel like you really belong anyplace. What other folks call home can never really be home to a slave because it's not yours, and you might be sold at any time.

But finding out my mama had been at Rosewood, and

now being here with Katie like I was and finding out I was blood kin to Rosewood's mistress, Katie's mama, who was my aunt—what a feeling of belonging that gave me inside!

This was my home!

A real home! A place where Mary Ann Jukes—or maybe my name was really Mary Ann Daniels, I wasn't sure how that kind of thing worked—really and truly belonged and could call her own.

It felt so good! To think that at first I had been angry. I could hardly believe I had been so blind to the good side of what Mr. Daniels' disclosure meant.

We didn't have long to celebrate, though, before another question reared its head again that we'd kept ignoring all along because we didn't know what to do about it. Just when we'd found out who *I* was, suddenly we realized all over again that we still didn't know who *Aleta* was.

Two days after Katie had taken the gold into the bank, we saw a buggy coming toward Rosewood. We managed to get Emma out of sight and Aleta clanging the hammer in the blacksmith's shop again. I headed for the clothesline as Katie made her way toward the house.

"Who is it?" I asked her as we walked away from each other. "Can you see?"

"I can't tell yet . . ." she began, "—oh . . . it looks like it might be Reverend Hall."

"What could *he* want?" I asked.

"I don't know," she said as she walked toward the kitchen door.

I don't know why, but I'd been nervous about the minister all along and didn't want to hang around too close. I was dying to hear what he wanted, but I'd just have to wait and find out from Katie.

It was the minister all right. "Hello, Kathleen," he said as he got down from his buckboard and he and Katie greeted each other in front of the house. "Is your mother home?"

"No, sir," answered Katie.

"It's been quite some time since I've seen her, or any of you, at church. I thought it was about time I paid a visit to see if everything's all right."

"Yes . . . yes, we're fine."

"Still no word from your father?"

"No, sir."

"You remembered to tell your mother what I said when I saw you that day in town?"

"Yes, sir."

From where I was I saw Reverend Hall glance toward the blacksmith's shed where Aleta's arm was probably already starting to get tired. When all this pretending of ours was over, Aleta was going to have almighty strong arms, that was for sure! The thought crossed my mind that they might be talking about her, and I wasn't so far wrong.

"Kathleen," said the minister, "do you remember my telling you about the man who had a drinking problem, whose wife and daughter were afraid of him?"

"Yes, sir," answered Katie a little slowly, unconsciously glancing down at the ground.

"Well, the situation finally became so bad," the minister went on, "that the lady and little girl left home. Nobody has seen them for a long, long time."

He looked at Katie, and Katie said his eyes were full of question.

"And . . . what happened?" she said.

"The man has sobered up because of it," said Reverend Hall. "He knows what happened was his fault and he feels terrible about it. But he hasn't heard from them and can't find them anywhere."

By now Katie was getting nervous as she listened!

"You haven't seen a lady with a little girl anywhere, have you, Kathleen?"

"A lady with a girl? Uh . . . no, sir."

"And if you did hear about anyone like that, or if you saw someone you didn't know or if someone came asking for help, you and your mama would come and tell me?"

"Uh . . . what's the lady's name, Reverend Hall—in case I see her?"

"Mrs. Butler," he answered. "Her husband is Hank Butler, who lives over outside of Oakwood. Well, Kathleen," said the minister as he climbed back into his buggy, "we'll be praying for your father and brothers. And I would certainly like to visit with your mother sometime. Will you tell her I stopped by?"

"Yes, sir."

As soon as he was gone, Katie came over and told me what he'd said.

"Do you think he suspects she's here?" I asked.

"I don't think so," she answered. "Even though he was asking lots of questions, he didn't have that suspicious look people sometimes have."

"Like the lady in the store," I said.

"Mrs. Hammond *always* has it!" laughed Katie. "But

now that we know, Mayme," she added seriously, "it seems like we've got to tell him . . . don't you think? Aleta can't stay here forever."

I didn't have an answer to that.

Katie went to fetch Aleta from the blacksmith's shed.

"Who was it?" asked Aleta.

"Aleta," said Katie seriously as they walked back toward me, "that was the minister from town. He was looking for you and your mama. He told us where your father lives. He said that your father has stopped drinking and is worried about you."

"You didn't tell him I was here," said Aleta, half in question but with a hint of anger showing through in her voice. I could see the old fire in her eyes like how she used to look at me.

"No," replied Katie. "But don't you think we should? You could trust Reverend Hall. He said your daddy—"

"I won't go back to him!" Aleta interrupted. "You can't make me. If you try, I'll just run away. You can't make me go back home!"

"But you have to sometime."

"Why? You and Mayme and Emma don't have to go back to anyone."

"Aleta, we don't have anyone to go back to. If we did, we would."

"Mayme's got a father too, and she's staying here with you."

"But she doesn't know where her daddy is. It's different, Aleta. Besides, her daddy doesn't have a home at all."

"Well, Mr. Daniels is nice. He's not at all like my daddy.

You can't make me go back. If you do, I'll run away. I promise I will."

Katie and I looked at each other and shrugged. Aleta could be mighty determined when she wanted to be, and now was one of those times.

We didn't know what was best to do.

The Man With the Funny Name

29

Paying off her mama's loan with the gold we'd found had put Katie on cloud nine. Even the uncertainty about Reverend Hall's visit couldn't dampen her spirits. It was all the better knowing it was the last loan and that there were no more surprises waiting around the corner, no more letters from the banker about having to foreclose on Rosewood.

Though Aleta was a little quiet for a day or two, Katie was happy and singing and smiling, and her cheerful mood made all the rest of us happy too, even if it hadn't been for my own happiness inside about Katie and me being cousins. Even little William seemed to catch the spirit of it. He was getting on to the age where he was trying out his legs to see if they could support his tubby little tummy and the rest of him. Emma was so delighted with everything he did and wanted to show us something new every two minutes it seemed.

"Look, he's gwine git ter walkin' any minute," she exclaimed at least thirteen times a day. "Look, Miz Katie . . . look, Mayme . . . did you see dat . . . did you see him! He's doin' it . . . he's doin' it!"

But every time it seemed like William was about to take off and walk across the room, he'd fall back down on his fat little rump. But it was funny watching him. He was so cute, babbling his baby talk and crawling around and getting into things. He was so curious. Everything he touched he wanted to put in his mouth!

One day about a week after we'd been to the bank, we were all in the kitchen laughing at William as he kept trying to stand up, then tottered a few steps before falling down again. Jeremiah had come out early in the day and was outside ploughing one of the fields because it was starting to get real warm and Henry said the ground was just right for turning. I'd just come back a while earlier from taking him some water and something to eat and now we were watching William when suddenly there was a knock on the door. At first I thought it might be Jeremiah since we hadn't heard anyone ride up.

It got quiet for a minute, then Katie walked to the door and opened it. I got up and followed her and stood a few steps behind her.

There stood a man neither of us knew. He was wearing a tie and a suitcoat even in the heat, and had a business kind of hat on his head. His eyes were narrow and squinty-like and reminded us of Mrs. Hammond when she was peppering you with questions. He was a man who looked suspicious. The stranger looked straight at Katie without smiling.

"I am sorry for coming to the kitchen door like this,"

he said. "I went around front but saw no one, and then I heard the voices in here."

"That's all right," said Katie. "This is the door we use most of the time anyway."

"Is the man of the house at home . . . uh, Mr. Clairborne?"

"No, sir."

"How about Mrs. Clairborne?"

"Uh . . . no, sir. She's away. But I am Kathleen Clairborne."

"Mrs. Clairborne would be your mother?"

"Yes, sir."

"Ah yes . . . I see. Well, I need to ask her about this," said the man.

He pulled something out of his pocket and held out his right hand. In the middle of his palm sat one of the nuggets of gold that Katie had given to the man at the bank. Katie recognized it immediately. She knew from the shape that it was one of the same ones. She swallowed hard, though her mouth was suddenly dry.

"Uh, why?" said Katie. "What about it . . . I'll, uh, tell my mother when she gets home."

"I understand she took this to the bank," he said. "Mr. Taylor brought it to me. I am an attorney and also the acting government deputy clerk for Shenandoah County. Among my duties is that of assayer. We have been investigating a theft of government gold that occurred during the last year of the war. Before I could process Mr. Taylor's request, I had to investigate further."

By now Katie's mouth was really dry!

"But that couldn't—" she started to say. She was going

to tell him that her mother had had the gold for years and that it had come from California with her uncle. But she stopped herself. She knew it was probably best to say nothing, since we hadn't wanted anybody to know about the gold at all.

"Uh . . ." she fumbled after a second or two, "uh . . . I'll tell my mama you were here," she said.

"All right, then, tell her that Leroy Sneed from Oakwood needs to talk to her . . . and soon," answered the man. "Please tell her everything I said, and that I will call on her again tomorrow. Good day, miss."

The man turned and walked back to his carriage.

"He was asking about the gold," Katie said as she closed the door and walked back into the kitchen.

"I know!" I exclaimed. "I heard him."

"He said he was from the government."

"How'd he find out about it?"

"Mr. Taylor showed him."

"I thought he wasn't supposed to tell."

"I think this man made him," said Katie. "He said the gold was stolen!—What if we're in trouble, Mayme? Maybe we shouldn't have taken the gold to the bank."

"It's too late to worry about that now," I said. "Besides, what else were you going to do—there's still the loan that's gotta be paid."

"What if the gold was stolen? What will we do then?"

"Do you believe the man?" I asked. "Do you think he's who he said he was?"

"I don't know," said Katie. "But I don't know if *he* believed *me*. And he said he was coming back tomorrow to see my mama!"

"Uh-oh," I said. "That's no good. You're not going to have anything more to tell him than you did today."

I thought for a minute.

"We gotta find out if he's really who he says he is," I said, "and if what he says about the gold is true."

"Why wouldn't it be?"

"I don't know. I just don't like so many people being so almighty interested in your uncle's gold, that's all. It seems a little funny to me."

All of a sudden Katie grabbed my arm. I looked over. Her eyes were big again, but this time with excitement along with a little bit of fear.

"Let's follow him, Mayme!" she said.

"How could we?" I said.

"On horses," Katie said. "He was going slow. We could catch him before he's halfway back to town!"

"What if he sees us?"

"We'll disguise ourselves. We'll wear some of my brother's clothes."

"Wait!" I said. "Jeremiah's still here. Let's get him to go with us!"

"All right. You go tell him and I'll go upstairs and start getting the clothes ready!"

I ran out of the house and toward the field where Jeremiah was working. By now Aleta and Emma were hurrying after Katie and drilling her with questions.

"We have to leave for a little while," said Katie as she started hurriedly changing her clothes.

"But what you doin' wiff dose feller's clothes?" asked Emma.

"I'll tell you later," said Katie. "It's just a little game.

We're trying to fool some people. We don't want them to know we're girls."

"Can I come too!" asked Aleta excitedly.

"I'm sorry, Aleta," said Katie. "We have to do it alone."

By the time I ran back to the house with Jeremiah, Katie had some clothes all laid out for me.

Three minutes later we were hurrying back downstairs to meet Jeremiah, who had been saddling three horses for us. Aleta was scampering along after us, still trying to change Katie's mind.

"Please, let me go! I promise I'll stay out of the way."

Katie knelt down and looked seriously into Aleta's face.

"Aleta," she said. "I need you to be very brave for me, and stay here and help Emma take care of William. Sometimes Emma needs somebody else to help her think straight and not get confused about things. Can you do that? Can you help Emma?"

"I'll try, Katie."

"Good girl! We'll be back as soon as we can."

THE SUSPICIOUS LEROY SNEED

30

POOR JEREMIAH! IT SEEMED HE WAS ALWAYS GETting roped into doing something for us that he didn't understand. Last year Katie had flown into town to the livery to get him to help her rescue me from William McSimmons. And now suddenly he found himself riding off with us after a man he'd never seen for reasons he knew nothing about.

"What you need ter foller him fo'?" he asked as Katie and I ran out to the barn to meet him.

"There's no time to explain, Jeremiah," said Katie, jumping onto Dover's back. "We'll tell you all about it later. Right now we just have to find out if the man who was just here is who he says he is, and why he's got my uncle's gold."

"Gold!" exclaimed Jeremiah. "Tarnashun, Miz Katie—I never heard nuthin' 'bout no gold!"

"It's not that much, Jeremiah," she said. "Just enough to get me and Mayme out of a pickle. And now some man has the gold and we want to know why."

"Dad burn, Miz Katie, dat's 'bout da blambdest—"

Whatever else he might have been going to say was drowned out in the sound of Dover's hooves as Katie galloped off toward town.

Jeremiah and I followed her in the direction of Greens Crossing and that put an end to any more conversation for the moment.

We rode hard for five or six minutes, then eased back. The man hadn't been going fast when he left Rosewood, just clomping along leisurely in his buggy. We had to be careful we didn't ride too fast and come right up behind him. So we kept watch as we gradually slowed, and about halfway to Greens Crossing we spotted him a quarter mile or so on the road up ahead of us.

We slowed our three horses to a walk and kept back just far enough that he couldn't see us. Every time I'd look over at Katie dressed in her brother's clothes with her blond curls tucked up into a big floppy men's hat, her eyes big and wide, I knew she was a little scared. But she had that determined grown-up woman's look in her eyes too. She sure had changed! If she'd have been a man, I wouldn't have wanted to argue with her!

We followed for another ten minutes until he came to where the road split.

Then, as we expected, he turned off in the direction of Oakwood. Katie and I looked at each other, both silently thinking about what had happened at the McSimmons place and none too anxious to go near it again. But we had no choice.

We passed a few people as we went, but we just kept going, looking straight ahead. A couple of men stared at us as we went by, but we pretended not to notice. I don't reckon we looked too much like men! Two blacks and a girl dressed up in men's clothes—I doubt we fooled anybody! We passed the McSimmons' turnoff without incident, saw nobody, and kept going.

As we got closer to Oakwood I recognized where we were. We stopped as we reached the edge of town. I could see the man's carriage on the main street straight ahead just disappearing past the general store, then turning off left on the street right after it.

Because of the last time I was there, I was a little familiar with the town and how the streets were laid out. As we started up again and rode slowly along the dirt street, I had the feeling every eye in the place was looking at us, though they probably weren't. We stopped by the general store again where I'd bought the lace, hoping the man inside didn't recognize me. I may have been wearing some oversized men's clothes, but I was still colored. There was no way to hide that!

We got off the horses. Jeremiah busied himself leading them to a nearby trough for water, while I went to the corner, took a step around it, and looked down the street.

The carriage we'd been following sat in front of a tall building down at the end of the street. It wasn't a house or a store. It looked a little like a hotel, though from where I was I couldn't see a sign on the front. The man had just gotten out of the carriage and was walking up a flight of wooden stairs on the side of the building.

I went back to where Katie was waiting on the walkway in front of the store, thinking as I went. If we were going to find out more about the man, we had to get closer and see where he was going.

"Hey, what are you doing there!" said a gruff voice as the owner of the store walked out the door. Quickly I turned my face away.

"Nothing, sir," Katie replied to him. "We just had . . . I mean, I had some errands in town."

"Why are you hanging about here . . . with them?" he said, nodding toward Jeremiah.

"I told him to water the horses, sir."

"Well, then, do your business and git, young lady. I don't want no coloreds hanging about in front of my store!"

Katie's eyes flashed with anger, but she swallowed whatever she was thinking and just said, "Yes, sir," then led us a little way down the street from the store.

"Did you see him, Mayme," she whispered as we went, "—the man in the buggy?"

"He's down at the end of that street there," I said, pointing to the side street where I'd gone to look. "His carriage is sitting in front of a big building and his horse is tied to a rail. The man walked up some stairs and went inside."

We got to the end of the street and I showed them the building and carriage.

"Why don' we go back roun' where we came into town," suggested Jeremiah, "an' den come at dat buildin' from dose woods dere on da other side."

"That's a good idea, Jeremiah," said Katie. "That way we can get away from that store man, and no one in town will see us."

We mounted up and rode back toward Rosewood. We got to the edge of town, then turned and led our horses on a street that led to the right off the main road, with the woods on our left. The street went along the outskirts of town with a few houses and other buildings along the way, until up ahead we saw the side of the building I had seen, with the street in front of it leading toward the general store and the center of town.

"That's it up there," I said.

"Let's leave our horses here and walk the rest of the way," said Katie.

We looked around to see if anyone was watching us, then got down, walked our horses off the road to the edge of the woods, and tied them to some trees.

"What you want me ter do, Miz Katie?" asked Jeremiah.

"I don't know, Jeremiah," she said. "For now just stay with the horses. I'm more concerned for you than I am for us. Just the sight of a black man makes some white men angry, and I don't want you getting in any danger. But nobody will hurt us."

"All right, Miz Katie, but if dey tries ter—"

"We'll be careful," said Katie.

Leaving Jeremiah at the edge of the woods that ran along the side of town, Katie and I walked slowly ahead toward the building where the man's buggy was parked on the street that ran at right angles to the direction we were coming from. By now we'd made a big wide circle almost back to where we started.

When we got to it, there were windows all around, but I didn't see any people inside, and I figured the man was still up on the second floor. Keeping next to the wall, we walked around from the back, then stopped at the corner.

I poked my head around real slow. The front of the

building faced the street leading up to the main street where the general store was. Now that I was this close, as I looked I saw that there was a small wooden sign hanging from the front of the building. I tried to read it but didn't know what it said.

"Come here, Katie," I whispered. She was up next to the wall right beside me. "Peek around and see what that sign says."

I stepped back to give her room. Slowly she stuck her head out around me and looked, then pulled back.

"It says, *Leroy Sneed, Attorney at Law,*" she said. "Then underneath there's another sign that says, *County Clerk—Assayer.*"

"What's that?" I asked.

"I don't know. But whatever it is, that's what Mr. Sneed said he was."

"This must be where that man at the bank brought the gold," I said.

We stood for a few seconds out of sight by the wall, then I crept back toward the rear of the building again with Katie following me. I hadn't seen anybody nearby, but we ducked down when we passed the windows just in case. A few voices were coming from upstairs.

Along the back and sides there was a landing all around the building where people walked from the stairs I had seen on the other side to the rooms of the second floor. We couldn't very well just walk around in plain sight and go up the stairs. They would hear our steps coming up the wooden stairs, and probably see us from the windows.

We got to the back of the building. I looked up at the landing from underneath. It wasn't that high above my head. If I could just get up there, maybe I could sneak around to where I'd seen him going.

"Katie," I said, "I'm going to try to climb up this post and get up onto that second-floor walkway."

"What for?"

"I think he's up there and I want to find out."

"Make sure he doesn't see you, Mayme."

"He won't know who I am. How else are we going to find out what's going on?"

"All right," said Katie.

"But I'm going to need to climb up and stand on your shoulders," I said.

"On my shoulders!" Katie whispered.

"Just for a second, until I can hoist myself up to the landing."

I reached my foot up onto a crosspiece of the supporting post and pulled myself up with my hands.

"Okay now, Katie," I said, "let me step onto your shoulders—get a little closer to me."

She got up right next to the post and grabbed it to steady herself. I reached my left foot up and gently put it on her shoulder.

"I'll try not to hurt you," I said as I eased my weight down, "but I've got to get higher."

"It's all right," she said.

"I'm stepping down a little more," I said, "—all right, hang on . . . here comes my other foot."

I set the weight of both my feet onto her shoulders. She wobbled some and I heard a little groan, but she held my weight.

Keeping hold of the post, I reached up as high as I

could. But I couldn't quite get hold of the crossbeam of the walkway above me.

"I've gotta get a little higher," I whispered. "Are you okay?"

"Yes," she grunted.

"I'm gonna give a little jump and try to reach up . . . here I go."

I bent my knees a little and then, as well as I could on a wobbly foundation, tried to jump. Katie groaned again and I knew my boots must be grinding into her shoulders. But I managed to get my hand up above the beam where I could grab hold. I pulled up with all my might and got my second hand over it, then pulled again. I was off Katie now and hanging free. My feet were swinging in midair, trying to keep my body balanced. I pulled and swung some more, then threw my right foot up over the beam and twisted until I could get the rest of my weight up.

Half a minute later I was climbing to my feet on the second-floor walkway, with Katie looking up at me like I was a monkey or circus acrobat or something.

"What are you going to do now?" she asked in a low voice.

"Wait here," I whispered down to her. "I'm going to see what I can see."

"How will I know what to do?"

"Just wait. I'll be back in a minute. If you think there's danger, run for the horses and skedaddle out of here. I can run faster than most men. I'll be after you at full chisel."

"I'm not going to leave you, Mayme. Remember what happened last time you said that to me. If anything happens, I'm staying with you!"

"All right, then," I whispered back. "We'll *both* be careful."

Leaving Katie below me on the ground, I crouched down to keep below the windows and crept on the walkway along the back wall of the building, past one closed door. I got to the corner and poked my head around an inch or two. Up ahead I saw the stairs that led down to the street in front. I heard the voices clearer now than before. One of the windows up ahead was open a crack.

I got down on my hands and knees and snuck toward it until I was right below the window, then stopped and tried to listen. The only voice I knew for sure was Mr. Sneed's, 'cause I'd just heard his an hour ago in Katie's house.

". . . the gold . . . don't know . . . lady wasn't there . . ."

"Who was?" asked another man.

"Some kid?" he answered. "Kind of a thick-witted one."

I thought I recognized some of the other voices too, but—

All of a sudden I remembered!

It was the voices of two of the men who had come to the house a year ago who we'd chased off with the guns! They were the same men who'd come snooping around again just two weeks ago that Henry had overheard at the livery stable talking about Katie's two uncles.

What were they doing here! And with the fellow Sneed?

As I listened, they kept talking.

". . . what do we do now . . ." one of them was saying.

"Still no line on Daniels."

"How much has the banker still got?"

"Don't know . . . lots more somewhere . . . when Ward left San Francisco."

"I say we go back and rough up the place . . . gotta be there . . ."

"Just let me handle it . . . see what the woman says tomorrow . . ."

If I could just get a look and see for sure if it was the men who had come to the house.

I took off my hat and raised myself slowly, trying to get one eye above the ledge of the window.

But at the same time on the other side of the building down on the ground floor, Katie had just been seen.

"Hey, you!" said a man, coming out of one of the downstairs offices. "What are you doing here?"

"I'm, uh . . . just waiting for somebody," fumbled Katie in her high girl's voice.

The man looked at her funny and realized she was a girl.

"Well, we don't want no loiterers around here," he said. "So beat it, little girl!"

Not knowing what to do, Katie turned and slowly pretended to wander off in the direction of our horses, glancing back every once in a while to see if she could see what was happening to me. But she couldn't because I was up on the landing on the other side.

By now I had managed to get high enough to see through the crack in the window. There were three men—the fellow Sneed . . . and I'd been right! The two others were the men who had come to the house! On a table in front of them sat one of the nuggets of gold Katie had taken to the bank—the same one Sneed had had when he came to ask Katie about it.

But before I had a chance to think what it all meant, one of the men glanced toward the window.

"Hey, what the—" he said. "There's a black kid out there watching!"

Sneed turned toward me.

"What's that window doing open!" he cried. "He was listening to everything we said!"

The other man jumped up and ran for the door.

I didn't intend to hang around. I leaped to my feet and bolted for the stairs!

The man was outside within seconds. But all he saw was the back of my heels. I was flying down the stairs two at a time, hit the street running, and sprinted straight ahead up the street away from Katie toward the general store, hearing booted feet tromping down the stairs after me.

"Hey, somebody stop that colored kid!" shouted a voice.

From where she stood behind the building, Katie watched as the man ran down the stairs. She didn't know what to do, since I was running away from her. But she didn't have time to think about it because all of a sudden a big black form ran past her toward the front of the building and slammed into the man as he reached the bottom of the stairs. Both of them sprawled to the ground and tumbled over each other.

"Why, you fool nigger!" the man shouted, yelling a bunch of profanities along with it. "Why don't you watch where you're going!"

"Ah'm mighty sorry, massah, suh," said Jeremiah, climbing slowly to his feet. "Ah wuz jes' chazin' mah dog what's got loose."

"Hang your blasted dog! Just get out of my way!"

By now the man was back on his feet and after me again. But I'd already reached the corner by the general store. I turned and glanced back. Even though Jeremiah had slowed them up, now there were two men running up the street after me.

I turned around the corner to the right and dashed past the general store the way we'd ridden a few minutes earlier. In the meantime, Jeremiah and Katie ran back to the horses.

"Jeremiah, you're in enough trouble," said Katie. "You take two of the horses, keep to the woods, and start for home."

"What about Miz Mayme?"

"I'm going after her," said Katie, jumping on Dover's back. "You listen for us. We'll just be a few minutes behind you, maybe less. But you stay out of sight. I don't want those men seeing you again."

With that Katie was off, galloping back down the side street that skirted the woods on the edge of town.

I got to the street leading off the main road, then turned right.

There was Katie galloping toward me.

"Mayme!" she cried.

"Am I glad to see you!" I said, panting for breath. "Let's get out of here!"

She reached down and I grabbed her hand. She pulled me up behind her. I hung on to Katie's waist and she dug her heels in and off we galloped again.

"Ride into town!" I shouted to her from behind. "We don't want them following us back to Rosewood!"

Katie must've thought it was a crazy idea to ride right

toward the men where they were sure to see us. But she went along with it. A few seconds later we were galloping past the general store again just as the two men reached the main street. They looked surprised to see us on horseback and galloping straight toward them. I heard a few bad words shouted at us as we tore past and they saw me sitting behind Katie.

"Hey . . . hey, stop you! Hey, you colored—what were you—"

But we were already past them and disappearing down the street past the sheriff's office and bank. I was glad the sheriff wasn't outside just then. We didn't want *him* getting too curious about us either!

"Let's get back to our horses!" I heard one of the men shout. "We've got to stop them!"

"Where are we going?" Katie shouted to me.

"I'll tell you when we get there," I yelled back.

People were watching us as we flew through town. I told Katie to turn left at the bank. We rode past the hotel where I'd looked for the job, then left on the street that ran alongside it. There were fewer people there, and I told Katie to rein in.

"Hurry, Katie," I said, "let's get down."

We jumped off Dover's back, then I led Katie and him off the street into a narrow alley behind the hotel, then around another corner and behind the building at the back where the man had shown me the room. There we stood, breathing heavily but out of sight from the street.

"Why did we come here?" asked Katie.

"I didn't want them to see us riding back in the direction of Rosewood," I said. "Now they think we're going out of town in the opposite direction. So if they follow us, they'll be going the wrong way. I hope they haven't recognized who we are."

"That was smart, Mayme!"

A few seconds later the sound of galloping horses thundered past in the street at the end of the alley.

"There they go," I said. "I don't know how long it will be before they realize we're not in front of them. But let's don't wait to find out. Come on!"

We left the enclosure by the building and hurried back into the alley. We followed it all the way to the other end and came out into another street I hadn't seen before. I didn't know exactly where we were, but we knew the general direction we needed to go.

We mounted again, trying to stay calm and not gallop and draw attention to ourselves, and made our way through a few more back streets until we came again to the other side of town by the general store.

The minute we were on the road and out of sight of any more buildings and people, Katie lashed Dover up to a gallop again, and we rode hard for a mile or two until we heard a shout from the woods alongside the road.

Katie reined in. A second or two later Jeremiah came up toward the road with the other two horses.

I jumped down from behind Katie, got on Red, and away we went again.

This time we didn't stop until we were back at Rosewood.

Mrs. Clairborne
31

THE MAN CALLED SNEED ARRIVED AT ROSEWOOD again the next morning, just like he'd said he would. We'd told Jeremiah what was going on and he said he'd come back out in case we needed any help. When Mr. Sneed arrived Jeremiah was out in the field with the big plough horse.

Knowing Mr. Sneed was coming, we were ready for him. We had three fires going and a couple of horses saddled by the house to make it look like more people were around. As soon as we saw him coming in the distance, I ran to Aleta, who was waiting in the blacksmith's shop.

"Now," I called out. "Start pounding, Aleta . . . but remember to make it irregular . . . and don't come out till I come get you."

She started pounding with the hammer on the blacksmith's anvil. When Sneed rode up and drove through the yard around to the front of the house, I was walking by with a load of laundry, and there was the sound of the hammering from the blacksmith's shop, along with smoke from the fire I'd built there, and the fire from the slave cabin.

I thought the whole place looked pretty lively. But he didn't seem to take any notice of anything. I reckon that was good. We didn't want him to think anything was out of the ordinary.

The biggest surprise of all was waiting for him behind the front door.

The plan that Katie and I had thought of the night before was probably even crazier than everything we'd done up till now!

After we got Aleta to bed, we were talking about the gold. If Mr. Sneed knew we had the rest of it, we knew he would try to take it all. Especially knowing like we did after yesterday that he wasn't alone and that the men who had been here twice already were in cahoots with him. But we didn't know what we could do to stop him from taking it. With him and those other men, they could do anything they wanted to us, and there wouldn't be anything we could do to stop them. If we refused or made them mad, there was no telling what they might do. The men besides Sneed looked real mean, like they wouldn't think twice about hurting us. We had to somehow make them think there was no more reason to keep snooping around and bothering us.

"We can't just give him your uncle's gold," I said. "Then you'd have nothing left at all."

"They're sure there's more," said Katie. "That's what Uncle Templeton said too, don't you remember—that they were sure there was more. From what you said you heard yesterday, they're not going to stop until they get it."

In a way maybe it didn't matter. If the man at the bank

wouldn't take the gold in payment for the loan, then I suppose it didn't matter how much Katie had. He might still foreclose on Rosewood. But then we realized that we didn't know whether Mr. Sneed was telling Mr. Taylor the truth about the gold being from a robbery. Katie said the gold had been at Rosewood for years, so it didn't seem likely.

The only conclusion we could come up with was that one way or another Katie had to keep hold of what gold she could. It was the only chance she had. She said maybe she could take it to somebody else in another town to sell it for money to give to the bank.

"Now I wish I hadn't given Mr. Taylor the biggest and best of the nuggets," said Katie.

"There's plenty more," I said.

"But the rest is just all little pieces and flakes and powder. It's probably not worth as much. I wonder if Mr. Taylor gave it all to that man Sneed."

"He only seemed to have that one chunk when I looked through the window," I said.

As we were talking about it, right about then's when I had my idea.

"If you could just fool him into thinking there *wasn't* any more," I said, "just like we're trying to fool him about not being alone here."

"Fool him . . . how do you mean?" asked Katie.

"Fool him about the gold too," I said. "Make him think there's no more so he and those men don't come around anymore and will leave us alone. Right now they think you've got more. So if you just say *no,* he'll be suspicious."

"What are you thinking, Mayme?" said Katie. "I can tell from that look on your face that you've got an idea."

I laughed. "You're right," I said. "I was thinking . . . what if you give him just enough to make him *think* you've given him all of it!" I said.

"You mean just . . . give it to him?" said Katie. "Give him the gold?"

"Just *some* of it!" I said. "Give him enough to fool him into thinking it's the whole thing."

"Do you think it would work?"

"I don't know. But if he thinks he's got *all* the gold, there's no reason for him to keep coming around. I don't know about the banker and the loan and all that, 'cause if he won't take the gold for the loan, you're still in a fix. But at least you'd still have *some* gold left."

"Except that Mr. Taylor's still got what I gave him," said Katie.

"There's no helping that now," I said. "First we've got to worry about Mr. Sneed. And I think we ought to dress you up again to pretend to be your ma."

"Oh no, Mayme—that was too hard!"

"You can do it, Katie. It's just one more time. We'll fix your hair even better and put rouge and stuff on your face to make you look older."

"Mayme!"

But eventually Katie agreed because she couldn't think of anything better.

That morning we went down into the cellar where the rest of the gold was still hidden in the lantern. We got a small old canvas bag from the barn and emptied out maybe a fourth of the gold into it, so that there was just about two inches of gold powder and a few small nuggets in the bottom of the bag. It felt funny scooping the gold out with our fingers and hands into the bag. It wasn't any different than the feel of sand and tiny pebbles. I wondered why it was so valuable.

Once we had the bag of gold ready, we closed up the cellar again and started getting Katie ready. We fixed her hair different and got her dressed, and put on some of her mama's lip rouge and powder and some ash smudges under her eyes to make her look older and stuffed a small pillow under her dress to make her look fatter. She was nervous, but she knew she had to do it. Emma and Aleta were curious and full of questions. We knew we had to get them settled down too!

When Mr. Sneed came, and after Aleta was clanging away in the blacksmith's shop, I came into the kitchen so I could listen and so I would be nearby in case something went wrong.

He watched me as I went inside, but then continued on around to the front of the house, stopped and got out of his buggy, and went to the door.

When the knocker sounded, Katie nearly jumped a foot off the floor. I ducked back out of sight in the kitchen and waited.

I heard the front door open.

Mr. Sneed seemed to hesitate a moment.

"Uh . . . Mrs. Clairborne," he said as he stood staring at the odd-looking plump lady who met him at the door.

"Yes," said Katie, trying to make her voice sound like her mother's. "You must be Mr. Sneed. My daughter told me you would be coming. Won't you come in?"

Katie led him inside. If her voice was shaky, I couldn't tell from listening.

"My daughter said you were inquiring about the gold we had taken to Mr. Taylor at the bank."

"Yes, that is correct," said Sneed. "As I explained to her, we think it may be part of a stolen governmental shipment . . . so I must ask you how you came by it, Mrs. Clairborne."

"I have a brother by the name of Ward Daniels," said Katie. "He was always something of an adventurer. He went to California in 1849 and was there for some time. The next time I saw him was just before the war. He was back in the East and had a small bag of gold from his prospecting in California. He asked me to keep it for him."

"Why would he have done that, Mrs. Clairborne?"

"I don't know. He seemed to be afraid of something."

"And you say that was . . . five years ago?"

"At least, Mr. Sneed . . . perhaps six by now."

"I see. And do you, ah . . . do you still have this gold?"

"All except what I took to—that is . . . except for what my daughter took to Mr. Taylor a week ago. I did not feel it was my right to use it, you see. It does belong to my brother after all. But times became difficult, with my fa—that is, after my husband left for the war. And now with all our slaves gone and only the few hired darkies we've been able to afford to keep on. He has had to go north to find work, you see, to help with our expenses."

"Ah . . . I see."

"I keep things going as best I can, with what he is able to send me. But it has been very difficult. Surely this does not look like a wealthy place to you, does it, Mr. Sneed?"

"Uh, no . . . yes, I see what you mean."

"That is why finally I had no choice," Katie continued,

and I could hardly keep myself from laughing to hear how different she sounded, "but to take some of the larger stones in to see what Mr. Taylor could sell them for."

"Unfortunately, Mrs. Clairborne," now said Mr. Sneed, "that gold may not have been your brother's at all."

"I thought you said that—uh . . . my daughter said that it was from a robbery from only a year ago."

"Yes, well . . . we are, as I say, looking into the matter. May I see the rest of the gold?"

"Yes, I have it right here."

Katie rose, walked across the room, and picked up the bag where we had put it on the sideboard. As she did, she glanced into the kitchen and caught my eye where I was hiding. I nodded and gave her a wink to tell her she was doing great. But her eyes were big!

Stay calm, Katie! I thought. *Don't let him see you looking like that!*

She took the bag back and handed it to Mr. Sneed.

He opened it and looked inside. He seemed surprised.

"This is all there is!" he said in disappointment. "This is hardly more than a couple hundred dollars."

"Except for what I took . . . except for what we took to the bank."

"I see. Hmm . . . well, I am sorry, Mrs. Clairborne," he went on, and I could tell from his voice that he was annoyed, "but I am going to have to appropriate this. If it is found that there is no connection between your brother's gold and the robbery, it will be returned to you. You're *sure* this is all of it? It was my understanding there was ten times this amount."

"Yes, sir . . . just one small bag," said Katie. "Perhaps he did not give it all to me."

"Hmm . . . as I understand also," he said, "Ward Daniels has a brother?"

"Yes, that would be my . . . uh, my brother Templeton."

"Right. Is it possible he has the rest of the gold?"

I heard Katie attempt a laugh.

"I seriously doubt it, Mr. Sneed. Whenever Templeton comes around here, he is asking *me* for money. If he ever had any gold, I imagine he gambled it away years ago."

"Do you know his whereabouts?"

"No, sir. I haven't seen him . . . uh, for some time."

"I see. All right, then. I had best be going."

He rose and walked to the door. Katie got up and followed him outside.

"Good day, Mrs. Clairborne," he said.

"Good day, uh . . . Mr. Sneed," replied Katie.

She stood on the porch until he was gone, then came back inside and collapsed into a chair.

I ran in from the kitchen.

"You were some pumpkins, Katie!" I laughed. "You almost had me starting to believe you were your mother too!"

Emma came bounding down the stairs a minute later full of questions, and I ran out to the blacksmith's shop to tell Aleta she could stop.

Katie and Mr. Taylor

32

THAT AFTERNOON KATIE TOOK A LONG NAP. THE interview with Sneed, after all that had happened the day before and the long ride to Oakwood and back, had exhausted her. After her nap we had another talk about what to do.

We still didn't know if Sneed was who he said he was. But we knew one thing—those men who had been here twice were after Katie's gold! Neither of us were too confident that they'd give up, even after what Katie had told them. The men who were involved with Sneed sounded mean, like they were the kind of men who would kill to get what they wanted. And gold could make people kill too. It got inside them and filled them with greed and hate and envy.

That night Katie looked up the word *assayer* in the dictionary.

"'Assayer,'" she read me out of the Webster's from the

bookshelf, "'one who examines metals to find their quantity, purity, and value.'"

"Maybe he is from the government after all," I said. "But that still doesn't explain what he was doing with those other men and why they're looking for both your uncles."

She put the dictionary away and we sat thinking.

"I still don't understand," said Katie. "If that man works for the government, why is he taking my mama's and uncle's gold? I thought working for the government meant you were honest."

"I don't know," I said. "I sure never knew anyone from the government in my life."

"He just *took* that gold, just like he took the piece Mr. Taylor gave him," Katie continued, more riled up than I had ever seen her about just about anything. "I don't know what to call it but stealing."

"Maybe just because he works for the government doesn't necessarily mean he can be trusted," I said.

"I don't know," said Katie, "but I was stupid to take the gold to the bank. Now it's gone."

"I don't know what else you could have done," I said. "You had to pay off your mama's loan."

"But it didn't pay it off," said Katie. "Mr. Taylor's still got it . . . if he didn't give it to Mr. Sneed. Just what kind of a name is that, anyway? I don't like it. And I don't like him! In fact," Katie added, getting that determined expression, "I'm going to go get it back."

"But you just gave it to him," I said. "That was our plan."

"Not from Mr. Sneed," she said, "from the bank. If Mr. Taylor won't put that gold on the loan, then there's no reason he should keep it. So I'm going to go get it back!"

And she meant it too, because the next morning she and I were off in the buggy to town again, and she was still acting mighty determined. We were doing so much traveling around lately that Aleta and Emma hardly thought anything about us leaving them alone now. But with all the goings-on and so many strange men around, we asked Jeremiah to come out again and be there when we were gone.

We got to town and went straight to the bank. Katie marched in without even waiting for me. I followed behind her a little timidly. Any other time I'd have waited outside, but I didn't want to miss this! And I was her cousin now too. Maybe I had the right to go with her.

She went straight to Mr. Taylor's desk. He looked up without expression.

"I've come about the gold," said Katie.

"You know about the problem with it, then, I take it?" he said.

"Mr. Sneed came to see my mother two days ago," said Katie. "He told her he had to take the gold because it was stolen."

"Precisely," said Mr. Taylor, "which means that the gold you gave me could not be applied to your mother's loan."

"My mother doesn't believe what Mr. Sneed said about the gold being stolen," said Katie. "He said it was from something that happened a year ago, but she has had it for five or six years."

"Be that as it may," said Mr. Taylor, "I'm afraid there is nothing I can do about it, Miss Clairborne. He is an attorney and the appointed governmental agent."

"He took all the rest of the gold too that we were going to use for expenses."

"I am sorry," said the banker. "That is unfortunate. But my hands are tied. As long as Mr. Sneed does not release the funds to the bank, I cannot apply it to your mother's loan."

"But what if he is just . . . *stealing* our gold?"

"That could hardly be. I told you, he has been appointed by the government."

"Well, I don't believe what he said," insisted Katie. "Did you give him all the gold I brought in?" she asked.

"Of course not, only the one piece."

"Where is the rest?"

"Still in the bank safe."

"Then I want it back," said Katie.

"Until I find out whether or not it was stolen, Miss Clairborne, I have a duty to—"

"It's not stolen," interrupted Katie, as close to getting angry as I'd seen her in a long while. "Mr. Sneed is not telling the truth. So if you won't take the gold for my mama's loan, then I want it back!"

By now her voice was getting loud and the bank manager was a little unnerved. Heads were turning and people were starting to stare.

"*Now,* Mr. Taylor," said Katie. "I want it back today. The bank has no right to keep it."

"Calm down, Miss Clairborne," he said in a soft voice, nervously adjusting his tie. "All right, if that is the way you want it, whether it is stolen is no concern of mine—"

"It's *not* stolen, I tell you."

"Fine, fine . . . please just keep your voice down," said

Mr. Taylor, now speaking in just above a whisper. "You can have the gold back and work out the legalities with the sheriff in Oakwood or Mr. Sneed or anyone else for all I care. But your mother's loan remains due in less than three weeks."

He rose from his desk, walked across the floor, trying to smile at a few people who were still staring from the brief commotion Katie's raised voice had caused, and disappeared behind the counter. Katie and I stood there in silence. The other people in the bank gradually returned to their business. However Katie might have tried to keep news about the gold quiet before, people had heard about it now!

Mr. Taylor returned a few minutes later.

"Here you are, Miss Clairborne," he said coldly. "But as I said, this changes nothing."

"That may be, but at least I have my uncle's gold back."

"Perhaps, but if the loan is not paid, I will have no choice but to begin foreclosure proceedings."

Katie turned to go.

"I understand from Mr. Sneed," said the banker's voice behind her, "that your father is working in the North."

"Yes . . . yes, that's right," said Katie.

"No one around here saw a thing of him when he returned from the war. When did he go up north?"

"A while ago," said Katie. "He had to find work. Good day, Mr. Taylor."

Henry's Ears Perk Up
33

Jeremiah and Henry were almost like our eyes and ears in town.

It's a funny thing about some white folks—not like Katie or Mr. Daniels and people like that, but white folks that can't see people of different color skin for who they really are. They figure if people talk and act different, that's the same as being stupid.

But like Henry said, it's who we are on the inside that matters, what kind of person we are, which direction we're moving, which direction we're growing, what we're making of ourselves, and whether we're letting God make us into the sons and daughters He wants us to be.

What I'm getting at is that people tend to look past folks like Henry and even Jeremiah because they're quieter and of a different color and maybe can't talk like they're educated, which neither of them were. And it makes them blind to how smart and shrewd and clever Henry really was.

So Henry managed to see and hear all kinds of things

that people never suspected because they ignored him, or, if they saw him, they thought no more of his overhearing them than they would if a dog was standing next to them. So Henry followed people without them even knowing it, and walked into stores and always kept his eyes and ears open, and folks never knew how he was looking out for us and protecting us and how much news he brought us about the town and what folks were saying.

One time he even told us something that Mrs. Hammond had said about us, which made us both laugh and get angry at the same time, and she'd never suspected he was even around.

But mostly he was watching for the men.

One day Henry saw Mr. Sneed come into town. So he left his work for a few minutes and followed him into the bank and pretended to be busy about something. But mainly he was trying to find out what he and the men might do.

When Henry walked in Mr. Sneed was already standing in front of the bank manager's desk in the middle of what sounded like a heated discussion.

". . . rest of the gold . . ."

"Please . . . keep your voice down."

"I want it."

"I gave it back."

"You what!"

"I had no choice. She was making a scene in the bank. Besides, I had no legal right to keep it."

As he listened, Henry ambled a little closer.

"I told you it was stolen."

"She says otherwise."

"You are a fool, Taylor, if you believe her. So where is it now?"

"I assume back at Rosewood. Where else would it be?"

"Well, that's fine, then I'll get it from them. I am still convinced that there is a great deal more . . . lady is lying . . ."

"I know nothing about that."

"That may be, but I intend to find out."

"—Patterson, what are you doing hanging about!" said Mr. Taylor to Henry as he suddenly noticed him.

"Uh, nuthin', Mr. Taylor."

"Well, then, if you have no business with the bank," said the bank manager, "get out."

Henry wandered out of the building but kept his eyes on the bank. He saw Mr. Sneed get in a buggy a few minutes later and ride off, but he saw none of the other men.

FORGIVENESS

34

FIGURING OUT WHO I WAS—THAT WAS ONLY HALF of what I had to contend with. Then I had to figure out who Templeton Daniels was. I knew who he was, of course. What I mean is that I had to figure out who he was—or maybe who he was supposed to be, who God intended him to be—in *my* life.

I reckon that's something everybody's gotta face sooner or later if they're going to be a whole and complete person. They've got to come to know themselves and who *they* are. Then they've got to figure out who their mama and papa are to them.

Some folks grow up without mamas and papas at all. But a lot more folks who have them grow up either hating their mamas and daddies or else feeling other kinds of bad feelings toward them. But we've all got to grow up and face the fact that God gave us our mamas and papas, and I don't reckon He did it by accident. I don't figure God likely does *anything* by accident. How could He if He's God? Even if they aren't perfect and did things to us that we didn't like, they're still God's children just like everyone else. So maybe they need our understanding more than our bitterness and anger.

I suppose that's the grown-up Mayme talking, remembering back to things I was slowly coming to realize at that time in my life but that I hadn't quite realized all the way yet. That's the way life is—you learn things slowly, especially things about yourself. Sometimes it takes a lot of years before some of the best things in life sink in. If you're trying to get rid of it, self-centeredness seems to gradually fall off you through the years. It's probably not because it gets easier when you get older, but that it gets easier because you've been practicing so long at it. So I'm not saying I realized this all at once. It was coming to me slowly.

I reckon what I'm trying to say is that maybe we all need to forgive our mamas and papas for the things they did that hurt us or confused us. I'd never held anything against my mama because I thought she was about the finest lady in the world. But now I came to realize that I needed to forgive Mr. Daniels for the resentment I'd allowed myself to feel toward him.

If he was my father, then maybe God wanted that word to mean something in my life. And maybe the first thing it meant was forgiveness. I realized that I could never altogether be the person God wanted me to be without it. I realized that lots of times wholeness as a person starts with forgiving others, and usually somebody close to you like a mother or father. At least that's what I found to be true for me.

I'd let myself be overjoyed to be Katie's cousin, yet I

began to see that I'd kept a few feelings of anger stewing down inside me toward her uncle. I don't know why. I knew I needed to forgive him. It really wasn't so hard to do either. People have such a hard time with forgiveness, just like they do with saying they're sorry. But I never saw that either one was so fearsome or so hard. Once I got myself out of the way and started thinking about how God looked at my father, and how God saw him the same way as He saw me and everyone else—with *love*—then I found that my heart had *already* begun to forgive him.

I think what might make forgiveness so hard for some folks is that they expect other people to be perfect. They especially never want anyone to do or say anything that might hurt *them*. But when it comes to looking inside themselves, they *don't* expect their own actions and words and attitudes to be perfect. And they make all kinds of excuses for themselves when they aren't. At least that's the conclusion I've come to from trying to figure myself out. I can be so cantankerously mean-tempered when I'm looking at somebody *else,* and so sweet and forgiving and understanding when looking at myself. Doesn't make much sense, does it? It seems like we'd want to treat everyone else the same as we do ourselves.

Anyway, that sure helped me see some of the dark spots in my own heart a little more clearly. And when I saw that my father *wasn't* perfect, and never had been perfect, and even that maybe God had never intended him to be perfect and understood a little better than me all the whys for everything he'd done wrong, it helped me to start seeing him differently. And then I discovered that maybe God looked at *my* imperfection in the same way, and that was a relief! God forgave me too!

And once I was able to forgive Mr. Daniels, then a new love for him began to open in my heart. When that happened, I felt that I'd finally begun to take some big steps toward growing up and becoming an adult. A lot of folks want to think they're grown-up before they really are. But growing up's got more to do with attitude than age. I believe I started to truly grow up when I knew I'd forgiven my father.

But no sooner had I done that than I began to feel guilty all over for what I'd done, for the things I'd said, for driving him away when he'd been trying to love me in the only way he knew how.

I got out the cuff link of my mama's again. I stared at the teardrop, as she always called it. As I remembered back, I realized that it had been when Mr. Daniels had seen me holding it that that peculiar look had come over his face, and that he'd looked at me that way ever since. That's the moment he'd known who I was, or thought he knew.

Suddenly I knew why. I stared down at the monogrammed TD and now realized that it didn't mean *teardrop* at all, but *Templeton Daniels*.

He had given it to her during that autumn they had been together.

She'd kept it all those years, even after being married to Mr. Jukes, as a reminder of the dapper white man she had loved so briefly and who had fathered her first child—me.

I thought back to the day when I'd asked her about it, and remembered the wistful, longing expression that came to her face.

"What's that, Mama?" I'd asked.

"Just a reminder of a long ago time, Mayme, chil'," she said, smiling in that funny way.

"What does that word on it mean?" I said, pointing to the TD.

"That stands for *teardrop*," she said. "It's a reminder of the tears of life that sometimes a body can't help, to help us remember that some memories are best left unremembered."

The words carried more meaning to me now than they had when I'd first heard them. I reckon I was just about woman enough by now to understand.

Mama'd loved him too, just like he'd said he loved her.

How sad it was that they never saw each other again, even though they kept loving each other. It made me cry. And my tears were all the more bitter because now I knew that I loved Templeton Daniels too, but might never see him again. It seemed like the forgiveness in my heart had come too late. What if his leaving this time turned out just like when he left Rosewood all those years ago? Was I going to suffer the same fate as my mama? Was this cuff link in my hand going to be my only reminder of my father?

I asked Katie for a chain, and after that I started wearing the cuff link around my neck. It would be a reminder of my teardrops too, the ones I'd shed for my dead family, and now the ones I shed for the father I had found and lost at the same time.

The day it finally dawned on me that I *loved* him, but that he was *gone,* I was sadder than I think I'd ever been in my life. When my family was killed, I was in shock and disbelief. Now I was consumed with an overpowering sadness that I didn't think would ever go away.

There was nothing else to do but cry. I had to be alone to cry the kind of tears I could feel about to erupt out of me.

I went to Katie's place in the woods. I stayed there two hours.

No Ain't No Answer
35

A FEW DAYS LATER WE WERE OUT PLANTING A field that Jeremiah had recently finished ploughing with new cotton seed when the men came. We knew instantly that they weren't in a friendly mood.

Aleta was in the yard taking care of William. The men rode up before she could get back into the house. Immediately they surrounded her with their horses.

"Where's your pa, little girl!" said one of the men gruffly.

Terrified, she just stood there, unable to say a word.

"I asked you a question, girl!" the man yelled. "Am I going to need to get down and horsewhip it outta—"

"Hold on, Jeb," said one of the others who had ridden over by the barn. "I see 'em. They're out yonder in the field."

Without another word, they spun their horses around and galloped off, leaving Aleta trembling and still standing where she was.

We heard them coming. But they were riding so fast there was nothing we could do but wait. The second I saw them, terror seized me. Even though there were only three of them, the reckless way they were riding reminded me of the marauders that had killed Katie's and my families. They came galloping straight across the vegetable garden we'd been planting, kicking up the fresh dirt and destroying the seedbeds and young shoots that had started to grow, then tore toward us across the nice furrows Jeremiah'd worked so hard at with his ploughing. It seemed like they were trying to do as much damage as they could. Even their horses looked angry.

"It's just a bunch of kids and darkies!" said one as they reined in close to us like they were trying to scare us.

"Where's Clairborne!" yelled the one who seemed to be the leader.

Nobody spoke.

"You all deaf!" he shouted with a menacing tone.

"I'm Kathleen Clairborne," said Katie, stepping forward.

"Yeah, well, I asked for Clairborne, not some kid. Who are you?"

"I'm his daughter. He's not here."

"Where is he?"

"He's away. He's up north."

"She's the one Sneed said the banker told him about, Jeb," said one of the other men, riding his horse over next to Katie and brushing alongside her. Even as he said it, he eyed Katie with a look I didn't like.

"Say, young lady," he said, "you look uncommonly like your ma."

"That's what people say," said Katie, staring straight

ahead and trying to ignore him, which wasn't easy to do.

"Except that you're a lot prettier.—Can't you look at me when I'm talking to you, girl! I said you was pretty. Don't you like that?"

Still Katie kept staring forward.

Now the man reached down from his horse and felt Katie's hair, then started running his hand slowly across her cheek.

Beside me I felt Jeremiah take a step toward him.

"Jeremiah," I whispered, "don't. She'll be all right."

"Cut it out, Hal," said the one called Jeb. "Time for that later when we got what we come for." Then he turned back to Katie. "Now, little girl, you listen to me," he said angrily. "It's your ma we want if your pa ain't here—or what she's got. And that is her brother's gold."

"I'm sorry . . . my mama isn't here either," said Katie.

"She still sick?"

"Uh . . . yes, sir."

"Well, maybe that's so, but I reckon you know about that gold too."

"I've only heard about it, sir."

"And you have nothing to tell us about Ward Daniels?"

"No, sir," said Katie. "I've never seen my uncle Ward."

The man let out an exasperated sigh, and it was obvious he was losing his patience.

"Now look," he said, "we're tired of fooling around. This is the third time we've come here, and we're asking peaceable-like. Fact is, Ward Daniels stole some gold from us and we aim to get it back. Your ma told Sneed there was no more, but you see—me and the boys ain't quite as trusting as Mr. Sneed. We don't believe him. And to tell you the truth, little girl, we ain't so sure we believe your ma either. She may be sick, but that don't stop her from being a liar. You see, that piece of gold the banker brought him, that's from what Ward stole from us. So we know Ward left it here, wherever he is by now, or even if he's dead. And there was a lot more than that little bag your ma gave Sneed. I don't know what she was trying to pull with the banker, but you see, we ain't convinced."

"What if . . . there isn't any more?" said Katie in a shaky voice.

"If your ma was playing it straight and don't know where it is, then we'll have to find it ourselves, 'cause it's here, whether you or she know it or not. And we aim to find the rest of it. It's ours. It don't belong to Ward, and it don't belong to your ma or pa or you neither. We ain't gonna take no for an answer. No ain't no answer at all."

Katie just stared back at him.

"So I'm asking you straight out—has your ma got the gold?"

"I'm . . . I don't know, sir. There's no more gold."

"All right . . . if that's the way you want it, you tell your ma she's got twenty-four hours to stop whatever game she's trying to play, or else to find it. Then we'll be back—noon tomorrow. You tell your ma that if she don't give us the gold, we'll take her place apart board by board if we have to. We're going to find it. I'm giving you fair warning. We'll be back . . . tomorrow. We'll have our guns, and whatever else it takes to find it. We'll ransack the place if we have to . . . we'll burn you out if we have to."

He spun his horse around and rode off and the second man followed. The third waited, then went up close to

Katie again and reached down from his horse to touch her hair and neck. "And just maybe I'll help myself to a little of this too, after we find your gold!" he said.

Then he laughed a horrible laugh and galloped away after the other two. Right then I think I could have killed him.

As soon as they were gone I went to Katie and took her in my arms. Every inch of her body was trembling.

"I don't know what we're going to do, Mayme," she said, tears filling her eyes. "We chased them away with guns once, and we fooled them once with me pretending to be my mother. But they're going to be prepared when they come back. They're not going to let anything stop them tomorrow."

What to Do
36

THAT PUT AN END TO OUR COTTON PLANTING for that day. What was the use of planting cotton if they were going to come back and knock the house apart, or even burn it down?

The first thing we had to do was tell Henry, and Jeremiah left for town immediately to do that. They both came out later and spent the night at our place in the barn. Even having Jeremiah there wasn't like I wished it could have been because we were all so scared. He and I didn't get the chance to be alone together at all.

Katie didn't know what to do. If she gave the men what was left of the gold, the bank would take Rosewood, and they might still not believe it was all of it and might do those other terrible things regardless. But if she didn't give it to them, they might destroy Rosewood before the bank could do anything anyway.

It seemed like there was nothing she could do that wasn't bound to have a bad ending.

And the minute they found out there were no grown-ups here but Henry, and that Katie's mama hadn't ever *really* been here at all . . . I could hardly sleep that night for thinking about the dreadful things they might do—like raping me and Katie and Emma and hanging Henry and Jeremiah. Right then, I was more worried about all that than I was the gold or the bank. The look in that man's eye when he'd come up close to Katie was a look to frighten any girl with an ounce of sense, and it sure frightened me.

I could hardly sleep a wink, growing more and more worried with every hour that went by.

Sometime in the middle of the night I got up and crept softly into Katie's room.

"You asleep?" I whispered.

"No," said Katie softly. "I can't."

"Me neither."

I got into bed with her.

"I don't know what to do, Mayme," said Katie. "Maybe I ought to just give them the gold. But I'm afraid they'll be just as mad because I lied to them yesterday, and it won't stop them from doing bad things. They don't seem like the kind of men that will be satisfied with it now that it's gone this far, especially if they find out I was just pretending to be my mama."

"Even if you give it to them, what if they still don't think that's all of it?"

"Then what's to be done, Mayme?"

"I don't know. Maybe it's finally time to tell the sheriff or some folks in town. Maybe some men would come out to help."

"But when it was all over, everyone would know."

"People are bound to find out sometime, just like Henry did."

"But the longer we can wait, and the older I get, maybe nothing will happen. If they find out now, especially with us having got into such danger, they'd take Rosewood away for certain and my uncle Burchard would find out and William McSimmons would find out where Emma was."

"I'd forgotten about that," I said. "He'd find out where I was too!"

"Oh, Mayme, it's too awful to think about! There's *nothing* we can do! And I'm so afraid for what they might do to us, especially to Henry and Jeremiah if they say or do anything to try to help us. Men like that don't like blacks, Mayme."

"I know, Katie," I said. "Believe me . . . I know."

"Didn't you see that rope tied to that one man's saddle? When I saw it I could only think of one thing. I'm so afraid for Henry and Jeremiah. And if they took them and tried to hang them, there wouldn't be anything we could do to stop them. Can you imagine how horrible it would be to have to watch them hang them, and watch them die right in front of us, knowing that when it was done they were probably going to hurt us. It's so horrible, Mayme . . . I can't stand it. And I don't think giving them the gold will do any good. Maybe we ought to tell somebody in town like you said. I would, except for the danger it would put you and Emma in."

Somehow we drifted to sleep. But when morning came it brought no answers to our dilemma.

And now noon was only a few hours away.

THE CLOCK TICKS DOWN

37

BY MIDMORNING THE TENSION WAS SO GREAT I could hardly stand it. Even Emma was quiet.

Katie went down to the cellar and came back a while later with another canvas bag about half full of what remained of the gold, including the nuggets she'd taken to Mr. Taylor at the bank. I could tell by the way she carried it that it was heavy. She clunked it down on the sideboard in the parlor.

"Well, there it is," she said.

"You gwine gib it t' dem, Miz Katie?" asked Emma.

"I don't know, Emma," said Katie with a sigh. "I just don't know. But I've got to be ready to give it to them if it seems like it'll help."

As Katie said it I could tell from the tone of her voice that she had about given up all hope of saving Rosewood. The bag of gold sitting on the sideboard was the only hope left—and now she was ready to give it away. She wasn't just scared, her voice was sad. It was like she had finally realized that our scheme had failed and she had given up.

Slowly the morning passed.

About eleven, Jeremiah jumped up from where we were all sitting together in the kitchen.

"I don' know 'bout da res' of you," he said, "but I'm gettin' me a gun.—Miz Katie, show me da gun cabinet, an' wiff yer permishun—"

Henry rose to his feet.

"Now jes' wait er minute, Jeremiah," he began. "We don' wants ter go git all riled. Ain't no good comes from killin', nohow. We ain't gwine do no shootin', not unless hit becomes a matter ob life er death, which ain't likely ef gold's sittin' at da root ob it—"

"Look, Papa," interrupted Jeremiah. "Dose men ain't gwine ter be feelin' too kindly tard Miz Katie when dey come, an' wiff respec' t' yer feelins' in da matter, I ain't gwine let dem hurt her, or any ob da res' ob dese girls. I ain't neber shot nobody in my life. But I's takin' one ob Miz Katie's guns an' I'm hidin' myself in dat barn, an' effen dey lay a han' on her or Mayme or Emma, or you either, den I'll shoot 'em. I'm sorry, Papa, but I ain't gwine stan' by an' watch dem do what white men sometimes does. Dey's carryin' rope too, an' dat fears me right fearsome. You can whip me later ef you wants, ef you an' me's still alive, an' I won't gib a squeak er protest. But right now . . . —Miz Katie, show me yer guns!"

Henry kept silent. I couldn't tell if he was upset or if he admired Jeremiah for his determination. Probably a little of both.

Five minutes later Jeremiah was on his way out to the

barn carrying a loaded rifle and a shotgun in his two hands.

I followed him outside.

"Jeremiah," I said, "please . . . be careful."

"I'll be as careful as I can be," he said. "I'll jes' bide my time till I see's what's gwine happen. I won't start nuthin'. An' Lord knows I's scared a da thought ob it all. So I's keep quiet, res' assured er dat, till I sees what dey's gwine do. But I ain't gwine let 'em rape Miz Katie, or hurt Emma or Miz Aleta or anyone—"

He paused a second and looked down into my eyes. It was a look that filled me with a feeling of comfort in the midst of the danger. There was almost a wild look in his eyes, but it was the look of love, not anger. In that moment I knew he'd die himself before he'd let anything happen to me.

"An' I sure ain't gonna let dem hurt *you,*" he said. "An' if dey lay a finger on my daddy, den I'll kill 'em."

Suddenly he stepped forward, leaned toward me, and kissed me on the lips, then turned and strode off toward the barn holding the two guns, leaving me standing there with my heart pounding about twice as fast as it should have been! It wasn't how I'd imagined the first time being kissed by a boy—with us worrying whether we'd live through the day.

But even with him holding two guns in his hands, it was mighty fine!

A Welcome Surprise

38

AT QUARTER TILL NOON WE WERE ALL THE MORE on edge and scared. Even Henry was sober and silent and just sat in a chair calmly waiting. He still had no gun. As was clear enough from what he'd said to Jeremiah, he wasn't a fighting man. He just sat there praying, though I could never have guessed the direction his prayers were taking. I reckon he would say that was his kind of fighting. We hadn't heard any more from Jeremiah since he'd gone out to hide in the barn.

Suddenly we heard a horse outside. The moment we'd been waiting for had come!

We waited. Still the bag of gold sat on the sideboard. I didn't know if Katie'd decided what to do or not. At a time like this, as much as we'd shared of our life together, what we were facing on this day involved decisions she had to make herself. Even a cousin couldn't help her now.

A tense minute went by. We heard the horse walk up and stop. A few seconds later a knock came on the door. It seemed so loud it nearly made us all jump right out of our chairs.

We looked around at each other. I could tell that Katie didn't know what to do. But she was the mistress of Rosewood now.

She hesitated a moment, then got up from the table and crept toward the door. Slowly she opened it.

"Uncle Templeton!" she exclaimed. The next instant her visitor found himself smothered in a tight hug of joy.

The words flowed like a wave of deliverance into the room. The rest of us let out big sighs of relief accompanied by smiles, and of course Emma started carrying on immediately.

"Hello, Kathleen," said Mr. Daniels. Even as he embraced her at the door, I saw his eyes searching past the entryway into the kitchen until they found me. He smiled above the blond hair of Katie's head buried against his shoulder, and I knew the smile was meant just for me.

"You came back!" said Katie, still holding him.

"That I did, Kathleen," he said. "Like I told you last time, I finally found that I cared about something other than myself. And now that I've got *two* girls to care about . . . or maybe *four,* I should say," he added, glancing toward Aleta and Emma, "I decided that I'd had enough of running away from my obligations. Every time a little responsibility gets too close, Templeton Daniels hightails it away. Well, maybe it's time I change that. I can't keep running forever. So here I am."

He stepped back from Katie and the two of them walked into the kitchen, Katie beaming with pride. Like he had so many times, he was looking straight at me and gazing deep into my eyes. Now I knew why. He was seeing my mother. And at last I wasn't afraid to return the look of love in his eyes.

Slowly I got up and went toward him. He opened his arms and I walked into them. He closed his embrace about me. I leaned my face against his big chest and stretched my arms tight around his waist. It felt so good to have him, my very own papa, hold me close, to know that he had loved my mama, and to know that I was no longer afraid of what it meant.

The whole kitchen was silent. Sometimes the reconciliation of hearts needs no words. I reckon this was one of those times.

I shed no tears right then. I'd spent my tears and they'd done the work that God invented tears to do—they'd helped clean out my heart and wash away the selfishness from it. So now I just stood, happy and quietly content to let my father hold me.

"You and me are going to have to have a long talk, Mary Ann . . ." he whispered.

I just nodded my head against his chest.

". . . a long talk about your mama, and about you, and me."

"We're so glad to see you!" said Katie, excitedly interrupting the quiet moment between us. "We're in trouble, Uncle Templeton. Those men I told you about . . . they're back. They're coming today, real soon . . . they said they were coming with guns! Jeremiah's outside right now with a gun. I'm afraid he's going to shoot them. We don't know what to do!"

Mr. Daniels stepped away from me and I fell out of his

embrace. A serious expression came over his face. That's when he noticed Henry standing on the other side of the room.

He walked toward him and stretched out his hand.

"I take it," he said, "that you must be Henry."

"Yes, suh," said Henry, shaking his hand.

"Templeton Daniels."

"Henry Patterson," said Henry with a nod.

"Well, I'm glad to know you, Henry," said Mr. Daniels. "From what these girls of mine tell me, you've been a mighty big help to them. I want to thank you. I should have been doing more myself. I'm still trying to learn a few things about life. I might be a slow learner, but I hope it's not too late for me."

"Ain't neber too late fer learnin' the bes' things life's got ter teach us, Mr. Daniels."

"And just what would those things be, Mr. Patterson?"

"Ter do fer others as we'd hab dem do fer us. Ah don' reckon hit gits much simpler dan dat."

Mr. Daniels nodded and smiled. "You are absolutely right. Well said. A worthy lesson indeed!"

Then he quickly became serious again. "How it is to be applied in a situation like Kathleen says you're in, however," he added, "sometimes that's hard to say. If I know these men, they're not the kind that will return good for good. In any event, I am most appreciative that you've taken it upon yourself to watch over things here. I hope we will be good friends from now on."

A little taken aback to have a white man treat him with such courtesy and even respect, and to take his words seriously, Henry didn't exactly know what to say.

In the meantime, Mr. Daniels turned to give Emma a smile and tousle Aleta's hair. "How are you two young ladies doing?" he said.

Even as he did so, Henry brought us back to the immediate hornet's nest Katie's uncle had ridden into without knowing it.

"Miz Kathleen's right 'bout one thing, Mr. Daniels," he said. "Dem men's comin' back. Dat's what I'm doin' here. Dey's after Miz Kathleen's gold, an' like she say, my son's out dere right now wiff a gun waitin'—"

But Mr. Daniels didn't hear the rest of what Henry was about to say.

"What!" he exclaimed, spinning around. "You found it!"

"Oh yes! I almost forgot," said Katie excitedly. "We found it, Uncle Templeton. There really was gold after all."

"Where?"

"In a lantern down in the cellar."

"A lantern!"

"Mama hid it in the base, in the oil chamber. But when I took it to the bank, a man called Sneed found out. He's supposed to be from the government, but we don't know whether to believe him or not. And then the other men found out from him."

"So they know about it?"

Katie nodded. "But they don't know how much there is," she said. "I only took some of it to the bank."

"Good girl!"

"But they said they were coming back today and that if we didn't give it to them, they were going to ransack the place. They even said they would burn us out if they had to."

"Looks like I got here just in time," said Mr. Daniels, taking in everything Katie had said.

He sat down with a serious and thoughtful expression on his face, then let out a long sigh.

"What's this about your son, Henry?" he said after a minute, glancing toward Henry.

"He took two guns, an' is hidin' out dere right now."

"Are the guns in the cabinet loaded?"

"Don' know, suh," said Henry, shaking his head. "But I ain't no man ter use er gun. Dat ain't my way."

Mr. Daniels thought a minute, then looked up at Katie.

"Where is the gold, Kathleen?" he asked.

Katie went and got the bag and set it down on the kitchen table. Mr. Daniels stared at it, then slowly smiled in a funny sort of way.

"A bag of gold," he said. "Doesn't look like that much, but it's what men dream of and will give their lives for . . . even kill for."

"But why, Uncle Templeton?" asked Katie. "*Why* do they?"

"I don't know, Katie," he answered. "It's more than just the value. Gold gets into a man's soul, and sometimes drives out everything else."

"Is that what happened to Uncle Ward?"

Mr. Daniels thought a minute. "The truth of it is, Kathleen," he said with a reflective sigh, "no. That's why Ward gave it to your mama, God bless her. The fact is, it was probably more likely to get into my soul than Ward's. Ward made a few enemies along the way, but down inside he was probably a better man than me. I couldn't see it for a long time, but now that things are starting to come clear in my brain, I can see that Ward probably followed more in Mama's footsteps than any of us. He was a good man."

His words of reflection quieted us all, until Emma spoke up.

"Is dat bag ob gold in yer soul now, Mr. Daniels?"

He thought for a moment, then began to chuckle at Emma's simple yet profound question.

"No, Emma," he said. "There was a time when it might have gotten in there. But no more."

He glanced around and let his eyes rest on Katie for a second, then on me.

"Now that I've figured out a few things about what's important, and now that I've found the two of you," he went on, "and I know how much that means, I don't want to lose you. No amount of gold is worth that."

"So what should we do, Uncle Templeton?" asked Katie.

"Why don't we just . . . give it to them?"

"What about the loan at the bank?"

"It's not worth anyone's getting killed over. We can take care of it. We're a family now. I'll talk to the banker. I'll tell him what's happened and about Rosalind and the rest of your family. Surely he'll understand. I'm certain he'll extend the terms a few months. I'll work. We'll harvest crops.—That's possible, isn't it, Henry?" he said, glancing toward Henry.

"Dat it is, Mr. Daniels," replied Henry. "Dese ladies here, dey picked dere own cotton las' year an' wiff all da lan' out dere, ain't no tellin what can be done."

"There, Kathleen, you see. It's just like Henry says. We don't need gold, we've got land, and that's better than gold. And we've got each other now too. We don't need that little bag of gold to be a family and to make Rosewood prosperous again. All we need is each other."

Suddenly the sound of horses from outside interrupted him.

Our brief enthusiasm vanished. Suddenly tension filled the room again. Unconsciously every eye in the room went straight to Mr. Daniels. Whether he liked responsibility or not, he was in charge now. He walked toward the open window and looked out.

"It's them, all right," he said. "There's four of them."

He thought a minute.

"All right . . . Henry, you take these ladies upstairs."

"What about you, Uncle Templeton?" said Katie.

"Right now I'm more worried about the rest of you," he said. "I'll talk to them and give them the gold. But I want the rest of you out of sight in case they're on a short fuse."

"Should we hide in the cellar?"

"I don't think there's any need for that. I'm going to try to handle this thing peaceably."

Reluctantly we all left the kitchen and Katie led the way with Henry upstairs.

In spite of what he had said, the moment we were gone, Mr. Daniels went to the gun cabinet, took out a rifle, loaded it, and walked with it back to the window, carrying a box of shells.

By then there were already shouts coming from outside.

SHOOTOUT
39

HEY IN THERE . . . YOU CLAIRBORNES!" YELLED the lead rider. "Time's up. We're back like we said we'd be. We're here for what belongs to us."

The voice they heard shouting back at them through the window, however, was not the one they had expected.

"All right, you out there," it called. "We've got the gold and we're not going to put up a fight."

The rider seemed momentarily puzzled as two of his partners rode up alongside him.

"That you, Daniels?" he finally called out.

"Yeah, it's me, Jeb."

"What are you doing here?"

"I'm here, that's all that matters."

"I figured you'd be back for the gold one day. Now I can settle my score with you for that money you cheated me out of."

"I never cheated you, Jeb. You're just a bad poker player,

that's all. You should never have called, holding just a pair of sevens."

"We'll see about that, Daniels," the man shouted back. "The way I figure it, I got the winning hand now."

"You're right, Jeb—no argument there. You got me dead to rights. That's why, like I told you, I'm just going to fold and let you walk away with the gold."

"Yeah, well, maybe it ain't that simple, Daniels, you ever think of that? Maybe it's gone too far. Maybe it ain't only the gold we want."

"What else could you want, Jeb? We've got nothing else."

"Yeah, well maybe we're just gonna take the gold *and* that pretty little girl in there for Hal here. And maybe I'll just kill you to boot."

"No need for all that, Jeb. I told you, you can have the gold. You don't want to get yourself into even more trouble than you're already in."

"Why should we trust you, Daniels? Ward lied to us. The woman lied to us. The kid lied to us. And you're all kin. We're going to take it . . . all of it."

From upstairs we could hear everything they were shouting back and forth. The voices from outside sounded angry. Whatever her uncle had said about staying out of sight, Katie couldn't stand it. She was so worried about him and scared about what they were saying that she couldn't stay put. All at once she got up from where she sat on the floor and dashed for the stairs. Henry tried to stop her, but by then Katie was out of sight.

"Aleta, Emma, you stay here with Henry," I said. "He'll make sure nothing happens to you."

I jumped up and hurried after Katie. By the time I caught up with her, she was in the kitchen listening to her uncle as he tried to talk to the men. We crept up beside him where he stood just to the side of one of the windows that was halfway open.

"What in blazes!" he said. "What are you two doing here?"

"I was afraid for you, Uncle Templeton," said Katie. "I wanted to be with you."

"Just keep your heads down."

We crouched beside him. But my curiosity finally got the best of me. I raised myself a little and snuck a peek out the bottom of the window. Just as I did, another man rode up alongside the fellow called Jeb—a fourth rider who hadn't been with them when they'd come before.

"They're all cut out of the same lying cloth," the new arrival said. "If the rest of you want to keep talking, that's fine. But I say we get this done and get it done the quickest way to make sure nobody lives to talk about it."

His voice was harsh and cold and cruel. The very sound of it made me shiver.

"Something about that voice seems mighty familiar . . ." said Mr. Daniels, more to himself than to Katie or me. Then he glanced over at me. "Keep your head down, Mary Ann!" he said. "What are you trying to do, get yourself shot?"

But I had seen enough.

It wasn't only the man's voice that made me start shaking.

Through the window I had seen a face I knew I'd never forget, with reddish hair and a thick moustache, and those horrible huge eyes of white. It was the man who had killed my family and trampled my grandpapa under his horse's hooves. A chill seized me and I began to tremble in terror as I sank to the floor. For the first time since that awful day, I thought we were all about to die.

Almost the same instant, beside me as he glanced out again, I heard Mr. Daniels say his name. The sound of it filled me with dread.

"It's Bilsby!" said Mr. Daniels. "What is he doing here!"

"Who is he?" asked Katie.

"He's the meanest cuss I ever knew," he replied. "I didn't know he was hooked up with the rest of them, but I should have figured it. He'll kill us all even if we do give him the gold. I may not be able to talk my way out of this."

I didn't have the heart to tell Katie who he was. And we didn't have long to wonder what they were going to do. Suddenly a shot exploded and sent the glass from the shattered window above my head tinkling all over the floor. The terrible man called Bilsby wasn't one for settling things with words but with bullets. He'd shed enough blood in his time, and a few more dead bodies weren't going to sting his conscience . . . if he had one at all.

"You girls get outta here!" said Mr. Daniels. "Bilsby's a guy who plays for keeps!"

He knelt below the windowsill, stuck the barrel of the rifle out the broken window, and fired back two or three shots. A rapid volley of gunfire came back at us and broke several more windows. Mr. Daniels fired back again and the room filled with the echo of loud shots coming from everywhere.

Katie was yelling and crying in panic—horrified to see

the house she loved being shot up, yelling at everyone, and terrified that someone was going to get hurt.

"Stop . . . stop!" she yelled. "Stop it!" But her voice was drowned out by the blast of gunfire and shattering glass and splintering wood and ricocheting bullets all around us. I don't know what it would be like to be in the middle of a war, but it seemed like this was it. Earsplitting explosions echoed from every direction.

Suddenly Katie jumped up from the floor, ran to the table, and grabbed the bag of gold. Then she darted for the door.

"Katie!" I cried.

"Kathleen, get back—" shouted Mr. Daniels.

But it was too late. Katie flew straight out toward the yard and into the middle of the gunfire.

"Stop . . . stop!" she cried in desperation, running toward the men. "Here's the gold, you can have it! There's no more . . . this is all there is! Just take it and stop shooting and leave us alone!"

Beside me, the rifle he had been using crashed to the floor. Katie's uncle jumped to his feet and tore through the door after her.

I stood and looked outside. One man was already down. Then I looked at Bilsby and watched in horror as an evil grin came to his lips and he raised his pistol.

I screamed in terror and dashed after them.

Running as fast as he could, Mr. Daniels threw himself on Katie and knocked her to the ground. The same instant a puff of white smoke burst from Bilsby's gun and a deafening roar filled the air.

He turned and saw me running from the house. I

glanced toward him and saw the same wild look in his eyes that had paralyzed me with fear a year before. He lifted his gun and pointed it straight at me. But then a second shot exploded from behind me. The same instant a huge splotch of red burst from the middle of Bilsby's chest. I saw the light of life instantly go out of his face and he crumbled from his horse onto the dirt.

"Katie, Katie!" I cried, running to where she lay partially covered by her uncle's body. My brain was in such a panic for Katie and the sight of the blood splattered all over her dress that I thought nothing of where the second shot could have come from.

But Jeremiah had seen it. He now walked deliberately out of the barn, shotgun in his hands. He was not looking at me but toward a second-floor window of the house, stunned at the sight that met his eyes. There stood his father with the rifle in his hands, still smoking, that had ended Bilsby's life.

"Let's get out of here," cried Jeb. "If they find us with him, we'll swing from a tree. I don't want to hang for the rest of Bilsby's murders!"

The bag had flown from Katie's hand as she fell. Gold and dirt and dust were strewn everywhere. With one last fleeting glance at the half-empty bag on the ground, the man called Jeb thought better of it, then spun his horse around and galloped away with his one remaining comrade, just as Jeremiah sent a barrel of buckshot after them.

I ran forward and knelt sobbing beside Katie. Blood covered her back and neck as she lay motionless. "Katie . . . Katie, please . . . please don't be dead!"

Then I felt her arm move and heard a faint whimper.

"Katie!" I cried.

She tried to roll over. "I'm . . . I'm all right, Mayme," she groaned. "I think I just fell."

I buried my face in hers and smothered her with kisses, hardly realizing that I was getting blood all over my hands and sleeves. For a second or two I was so happy to find she wasn't hurt that it didn't occur to me to wonder why there was so much blood.

Slowly the truth dawned on me. I leaned back onto my knees and now took in the horrible sight. The blood splattered on Katie's dress wasn't hers at all. It was the blood whose origins Katie and I shared, the blood of the *Daniels* name.

As Katie struggled to get out from under him and to her feet, Templeton Daniels lay unmoving on the ground, with the bullet from Bilsby's gun now lodged about an inch from his heart.

Vengeance Comes to Rosewood

40

I was still kneeling over Katie and her uncle when Henry emerged from the house, followed by Emma and Aleta. He and Jeremiah approached each other and stood gazing into each other's eyes a second or two, then silently embraced. Whatever they said in those moments together, I never knew. One thing I did know—Jeremiah realized what running downstairs to get that rifle had cost his father inside, and knew the sacrifice and heart-aching pain it had taken for him to pull the trigger.

When news gradually spread in the coming weeks through Shenandoah County that the marauder Bilsby was dead, and that it was the soft-spoken Henry Patterson from the Greens Crossing livery stable who had exacted the Lord's vengeance on him, Henry was a hero throughout the whole region, black though he may have been. In Henry's own eyes, however, what he had done had been born out of necessity not heroism. Though he never regretted his action, he would carry the grief for the rest of his days that he had had to take the life of one of the Lord's own.

From that day onward, if it was possible, Jeremiah held his father in even higher respect than before.

Slowly they came toward us.

By now Katie and I realized the truth. Both stained with his blood, still warm, we were sobbing and weeping over the form of our uncle and father that lay facedown in the dirt.

Henry stooped down and rolled him partially onto his side. His eyes were closed. A trickle of blood oozed out of the side of his mouth.

"Hit don' look good," mumbled Henry. "He's hurt bad."

He glanced up at us. Emma and Aleta were by then slowly approaching with expressions of awe and fearful curiosity.

"You girls, you don' need ter be lookin' at no dead man's face," said Henry, "effen dat's what dis is.—Jeremiah," he said, glancing up at his son, "you git t' town an' bring da doc. Ef he hesitates, you tell him hit's a white man. You git him here soon, boy. Don' take no fer an answer."

Jeremiah ran for the barn.

"—You ladies," said Henry again, "git back. Y'all can't do him no good now. He an' dose other two layin' dere—dey's in da Lord's han's now."

We stood and stepped slowly back, still weeping. We tried to make our way toward the house but were unable to tear our eyes away from the dreadful sight of Templeton Daniels lying so still on the ground in his own blood.

Henry now stood too and slowly walked to where Bilsby lay. He stooped down to see for sure whether he was dead.

He was.

"Well, I reckon you's gone ter da place," he said softly, and I could just barely make out his words, "where ye'll see effen da Lord can do somefin more wiff you by use er his far dan he was able ter eccomplush here wiffout it. I pray you won' be so muleheaded as you wuz on dis side ob dat ole ribber when da lovin' hand er dat far's flame bites in ter yer sowl an' opens yer eyes t' what you hab been. Whateber yer fate now, da Lord know what you needs an' what you deserves, an' He'll gib you both, 'cuz on dat side dey'll be da same."

Then he bowed his head and closed his eyes. I knew he was praying. All my life I wished I could have heard what dear old Henry was saying to God over the body of the man he had killed to save my life and Katie's. But I never did. And somehow I didn't think I ought to ask. When he rose a minute later, there were tears in his eyes. It was one of the few times I'd ever seen a man cry.

Then he walked over to the body of the man who had looked at Katie in the field the day before with such a lecherous grin. He wouldn't be looking at anyone like that ever again. He was dead too, from Mr. Daniels' rifle.

Despondently we stumbled into the house. Katie was still sobbing and babbling for her uncle. Though I had always been the practical one, I wasn't in much condition to be practical right then and I couldn't still the stream of tears pouring from my own eyes.

Now it was Emma who showed that she was made of

tougher stuff than some people thought. It was her turn to take charge.

"You two sit down right dere," she said. Her voice was tender, calm, and motherly. "Me and Miz Aleta, we's git yous cleaned up an' feelin' better in no time.—Miz Aleta, you go git dat tub upstairs fillin' wiff water, an' I be along t' help you directly."

As Aleta did what Emma had told her, already Emma was gently wiping at Katie's face with a wet cloth from the sink, wiping at the dust and blood and tears. "Dat's jes' fine, Miz Katie," she said. "You cry all you wants, 'cuz it feels good t' cry an' you jes' go right ahead. But meantime, we's gwine git a nice bath fer you and den you too, Miz Mayme."

When she had Katie's face wiped off, she went to the pump and cleaned the cloth with fresh water and then began washing my face too and talking to us both like she talked to William. Right then it felt good. I didn't want to have to think. I just sat there and let Emma wash my face and arms and dab cool water over my eyes and cheeks like she was being a mama to both of us.

Aftermath of Death

41

Emma managed to get Katie cleaned and into new clothes and put her to bed. Thankfully she was able to go to sleep almost immediately. That was one of Katie's great blessings—she could almost always sleep.

Emma insisted that I bathe too. But the water from Katie's bath had a slight color of red in it from the blood, and I just couldn't get in and use the same water like we usually did.

It took a while to drain it and lug up new water. By then I was about through crying, though I still let Emma mother me. It was a relief to do what somebody else said for a change. As she was pouring water over my head and shoulders and washing me in the tub, Emma said nothing about the whipping scars on my back. Whether she was shocked like Katie had been the first time she saw them, I don't know. I wondered whether Emma had ever been whipped like I had.

When I was done I got dressed. "Thank you, Emma," I

said, trying to smile. "That felt so good."

"Dat jes' fine, Miz Mayme," she said. "Eberthin's gwine git better by'n by."

I couldn't have slept like Katie. But neither could I go outside where the three bodies were still lying.

A little while later, the doctor came with Jeremiah. I couldn't help looking out now and then. I was terrified and curious at the same time. He and Henry pulled the two dead bodies off to the side of the yard, then a few minutes later the three of them carried Mr. Daniels into the kitchen.

"Where can we lay him?" asked the doctor, glancing around as they struggled to hold the limp body.

They looked at me. Since Katie was asleep, I reckoned I was the only kinfolk of the Clairbornes left, though the doctor didn't know it. So I figured it was my place to answer.

"There's a big couch in the parlor," I said. "Or there's beds upstairs."

"No, we don't want to carry him upstairs in his condition."

"You mean he's alive!" I exclaimed.

"Just barely," said the doctor, "and hanging on by less than a thread. Show me the parlor."

As I led the way, I couldn't help wondering what he thought to see so many coloreds in the house without sight of any familiar Clairborne face.

"And who is this fellow again?" he asked as they eased Katie's uncle down onto the couch.

"Mistress Clairborne's brother, suh," said Henry.

"Is he the only one who's hurt? What about the rest of them?"

"Yessuh—dey's all fine. Where's Miz Clairborne, Miz Mayme?"

"Upstairs," I answered.

"What about Richard?" asked the doctor.

"Mr. Clairborne's away, sir—he's up north," I said quickly. "But Mistress Clairborne's fine . . . she's asleep upstairs."

The doctor nodded and seemed satisfied.

"Well, as soon as we're done here," he said, speaking again to Henry, "I'll ride over to Oakwood and send the sheriff out for those two bodies. You got any idea who they are, Henry?"

"No, suh."

"I do," I said. "The man with the reddish brown beard is called Bilsby."

"That's Bilsby!" exclaimed the doctor. "How do you know?"

"Mr. Daniels said he recognized him. I heard him say so just before the shooting started."

The doctor let out a low whistle.

"Bilsby! This is going to cause quite a stir!" he said. "They've been looking high and low for him. Sheriff Jenkins is going to be mighty interested to hear this! There might even be a reward for all I know. This Daniels fellow shoot him?"

His question wasn't directed to anyone in particular. The doctor still didn't seem to know what to make of the fact that he was standing and talking to a roomful of blacks and one little white girl. The rest of us glanced around at each other, but no one answered him.

"'Bout dem two bodies, Doc," said Henry. "Don't

trouble yerse'f—Jeremiah an' me, we'll load 'em into one ob Mistress Clairborne's wagons an' take 'em ter town ourse'ves. We don' want dese yere ladies havin' dem layin' dere no longer'n need be."

"Suit yourself," said the doctor. "Just the same, the sheriff's going to want to talk to you about what happened."

"Yessuh."

"Bilsby," he repeated, shaking his head. "I can't believe it.—All right, I'll go get my bag. And you," said the doctor, looking at me, "I'm going to need some boiling water."

"What are you going to do?" I asked, probably a little too eagerly. I had been jumping up and down inside with questions ever since he'd said Mr. Daniels was alive.

"I'm going to see if I can get that slug out of his chest," the doctor answered.

"How?" I asked.

"How do you think—dig it out with a knife. It'll probably kill him," he added, "but if I don't, close to the heart like that, it'll kill him eventually anyway."

The thought of him cutting open Mr. Daniels' chest with a knife was almost more than my stomach could bear right then. His words silenced me. Emma saw the look on my face and led me away. We went into the kitchen to stoke the fire and get some water heating.

The doctor returned a few minutes later. He walked through the kitchen carrying a small black bag and disappeared into the parlor. I didn't know what to do, so I just stood at the stove watching the water in the pot. But it didn't seem any too anxious to boil. Water never does when you're staring at it.

About five minutes later the doctor came back. He

wasn't carrying his bag this time and his sleeves were rolled up.

"He came to," he said to me and Emma and Jeremiah as we stood there together. "He's mighty weak. I'm not sure I can do him any good. But he's asking for somebody called Mary Ann. He says before I start he wants to talk—"

I don't know what else the doctor said. I was already running toward the parlor with tears of happiness streaming down my cheeks!

Words of Love
42

SLOWLY I APPROACHED THE COUCH AND KNELT on the floor beside it. I wasn't worried about the blood now. Seeing Mr. Daniels' eyes open a crack and an attempted smile on his lips as he saw me melted my heart. I laid my head on his neck and put my arms around him, sobbing like a baby.

"Hey, little girl," he croaked, though his voice was barely more than a whisper. "I told you that you and I were going to have a talk together."

"Oh, Papa!" I said. "I can't help crying. I thought you were . . ."

"I know . . . I thought so too," he said. He tried to laugh but couldn't. "But I wasn't quite ready to go yet. . . . I had a few more things . . . that I wanted to say to you."

Right then I couldn't have said a word if my life depended on it! I couldn't stop crying!

"I'm . . . I'm sorry I left," he said. "It was . . . wrong of me. Always been too independent for my own good . . . me and responsibility were never much companions . . . why I kept moving around. When I met your mother . . . thought I was ready to settle down. But then I lost her . . . running ever since . . . running from having to face the memories . . . felt like I'd failed her. . . ."

He closed his eyes and I knew the guilt was killing him inside.

"Ran for all those years . . . tried to forget. . . . Then to discover I had a daughter . . . I was so happy . . . yet terrified. Part of me said I should keep running. Yet the look of your face reminded me of your mama. I'm sorry to say . . . listened to the first voice . . . had to sort things out, had to think. . . ."

"Papa, please don't tire yourself out talking," I said.

"All those years," he struggled to continue, ". . . consumed with thoughts of your mama . . . when I found out she had been killed . . . I couldn't . . . more than I could bear . . . suddenly realized that I had a lovely daughter, Lemuela's gift . . . maybe her gift to me."

He stopped for a moment, breathing in and out slowly.

"Do you know what your mother's name means, Mary Ann?" he said finally.

I shook my head.

"*Devoted to God* . . . told me on one of our walks in the woods . . . I thought of that . . . realized she had been a gift to me . . . and you were a gift to us both . . . kept thinking of your face and your smile . . . so much like your mama's."

He looked away. A tear fell from one eye. His voice was soft and weak. I wanted to tell him to stop, to save his strength for what the doctor had to do. But as hard as it was to see him suffer, I *wanted* to hear it. I wanted to know all there was to know. But his words only made my tears flow all the faster. It's a helpless feeling to cry and not be able to stop.

"I loved her, Mary Ann," he said. "I loved her all my life."

"I know," I whispered through my tears.

"And now . . . now at last I'm going to be able to tell her so myself. . . ."

His words were breaking my heart!

"I'll tell her that I found you . . . how beautiful her daughter is . . . that we didn't have much time together . . . but . . . enough time to know at last that we loved each other."

"Oh, Papa . . . I can't bear to hear you talk so," I wailed. "The doctor says—"

Again the faint sound of a laugh sounded from his throat.

"The doctor's a fool if he thinks he's going to save me," he said. "That's his job . . . rouse people's hopes . . . knows as well as I do I'm dying. Look in his eyes . . . he knows. . . ."

"Oh, Papa . . . please!"

"It's all right, Mary Ann . . . nothing to fear. I'm at peace. For the first time in my life . . . because I have you. . . . Wish we could have more time . . . wanted to take you to Charlotte . . . buy you a new dress—"

He coughed weakly and lay back on the pillow and took a few halting breaths, trying to gain the strength to continue.

"I can go to her now," he said, "and I can ask her forgiveness for not coming to find her."

"You didn't know, Papa," I said, trying to breathe in and steady my voice. "You didn't know where she was."

". . . could have tried harder . . . should have forced Richard to tell me. God gave me one of the loveliest of women to love, and yet I—"

His voice caught.

"But you did love her, Papa. You said so yourself."

"Yes, and I'll be able to tell her now . . . she'll forgive me too . . . kind of woman she was."

"Yes, Papa . . . of course she will forgive you. I'm sure she already has."

"So . . . so when I'm gone," he went on, trying with effort to lift his head and turn so that he could look at me, "you try to be happy, Mary Ann, knowing that your father and mother are together . . . that they love each other . . . that they both love you."

"I will . . . I will, Papa," I said, beginning to cry all over again.

He closed his eyes. His face was so pale.

". . . daughter to make a man proud . . . Mary Ann."

He lay back on the pillow, breathing more easily, though it came in such shallow breaths I could tell he was laboring. It was obvious that he was struggling to stay conscious. I was afraid.

After a few more minutes, he said, "And take care of Katie when I'm gone . . . all she has left . . . her kin now . . ."

"I will, Papa," I said.

"Stay with her, Mary Ann . . . watch after her . . . till

she's grown and . . . some man comes to love her and take care of her."

"I will."

"Promise me you'll take care of Katie, for Rosalind's sake . . . and that you'll remember that I love you . . . and that I loved your mother. . . ."

"I will . . . I will, I promise," I sobbed.

Again he closed his eyes. When he next spoke his voice was so weak I could just faintly hear him. I had to put my ear up next to his mouth to make out his words.

". . . almost forgot," he was saying, ". . . my pocket . . . saved it all these years . . . reminder of her . . . Want you to have it . . . help you remember the father who loved you . . . get it . . . vest pocket . . ."

I reached into the pocket of his waistcoat that the doctor had unbuttoned to get to his chest. Inside I felt something with my fingers. I pulled it out and saw the identical matching cuff link to the one that was hanging around my neck.

He reached out with a feeble hand and took my hand and closed it around the cuff link.

"Mary Ann," he said, "one last favor . . ."

"Anything, Papa."

"Kiss me . . . want to feel the kiss of my daughter before I go to her mama."

I wiped my eyes, though my cheeks were dripping, then bent down and kissed him. His lips were cool and clammy.

He smiled faintly.

". . . go in peace now," he whispered, ". . . love you, Mary Ann . . . love you . . ."

"I love you, Papa," I said softly into his ear.

"I'll tell . . . take care of . . . always remember . . ."

His eyes had closed again and I knew he had finally drifted out of consciousness. I was terrified he might be dead.

I stood up, wiped at my eyes, but it did no good, and went for the doctor.

The Operation
43

I KNEW MY EYES WERE RED AS I WALKED BACK INTO the kitchen. There stood Henry, Jeremiah, Emma, and Aleta all silent, every eye on me, and the doctor awkwardly waiting.

The moment I appeared, he sort of nodded, then disappeared toward the parlor again. Without thinking I walked toward Jeremiah and a moment later found myself weeping in his arms.

It was Emma's voice, so suddenly practical in the midst of our crisis, that finally brought me back to the present.

"Da water's boilin', Mayme," she said.

I stepped back and turned toward her.

"Does you know what we's 'pozed ter do?"

"No, Emma, I don't," I said. "But I don't think I can bear to go back in there right now. Would you mind asking the doctor what he needs?"

"I kin do dat, Miz Mayme. You jes' set yer mind t' ease

an' I'll take care ob everythin'."

She was already on her way following the doctor toward the makeshift hospital in the parlor. I went the other direction and walked outside.

The fresh air felt good on my hot face. I was full of so many emotions I couldn't think. I just had to walk. But I couldn't go anywhere. I had to stay close in case they needed me or there was any change. And I couldn't go toward the barn because I didn't want to look at the two dead bodies. So I walked back and forth between the front and the back of the house. How long I walked I don't know. It might have been twenty minutes, it might have been an hour for all I could tell. My mind was numb.

Finally I went back inside. The others were still all silently standing and milling around in the kitchen. All except for Emma, who was bustling about, face sweating, sleeves rolled up. As I came in she was rinsing some cloths under the water in the sink while Aleta pumped the pump, rinsing blood out of them. Then Emma dumped them in the tub of water boiling on the stove and disappeared into the parlor again.

Four or five minutes later the doctor appeared with Emma following behind him. He was holding his surgical knife and wiping it with a white cloth. Both were stained with blood. My stomach lurched and I looked away.

He cleaned up at the sink, then went back to get his bag and coat. Ignoring the rest of us, he nodded to Henry as he walked to the door. Henry followed him. The doctor didn't know that the man he had just operated on was my father. He couldn't possibly know how desperate I was for any news of his condition.

I stepped next to the window from which broken bits of glass still lay strewn all over the floor and strained to listen.

". . . got the slug out . . ." he was saying. I saw him hand something to Henry.

"Doesn't look good . . . hasn't lost that much blood, but . . . too close to the heart . . ."

Henry nodded and said something I didn't hear.

". . . did what I could . . . wouldn't hold out much hope . . ."

They stopped beside his buggy. He turned to face Henry and, at the same time, turned a little more toward the house so I could hear him better.

"I got him bandaged pretty good and gave that dimwitted girl some instructions," he said. "When Mistress Clairborne is up, you tell her what I've said . . . about all we can do is try to make him comfortable. If he goes when you're here, you and your son get the body out of there and bring it to me. Get him out of the house as soon as you can. We don't want them seeing it go stiff and cold. I'll come back tomorrow in the off chance he survives the night. But I'll wait a day or two before talking to the family about burying arrangements . . . don't want to alarm them yet. You'll be along with the other two bodies?"

"We'll git dem right away, Doc."

"All right—tell the sheriff he can talk to me about it if he wants, but you saw it, I didn't."

He climbed into his buggy, took the reins, flicked them a couple of times and called out to his horse, and bounced off toward town.

Henry came back in and motioned to Jeremiah. They

walked toward the barn. Jeremiah opened the barn doors and they began to hitch up one of Katie's wagons. I stepped away from the window. I didn't want to watch them load the two dead men.

A few minutes later I heard the wagon clattering out of the yard, and Jeremiah walked back inside.

THE VIGIL

44

AS SOON AS THE ECHO FROM THE WAGON DIED away in the distance, Rosewood became silent as a tomb.

It felt like a tomb too. In the center of its biggest and nicest room lay a man who was, to all appearances, already dead. And not just any man . . . he was my father and Katie's uncle. It was intolerable to remain inside. But where else was there to go? The life had left the place. Yet there was no life anywhere else.

Eventually Katie woke up. At first she was overjoyed to find out that her uncle was alive. But after I had told her everything, especially what I'd overheard the doctor say, we had a long cry together.

For the rest of the day we didn't know what to do with ourselves. Every time we went past the parlor we couldn't help glancing into the room where he lay so lifeless and quiet and still. It was awful to look at him, face white, shirt torn away, and a big bandage over his chest with stains of red showing through.

But we *wanted* to look. We loved him.

Somehow the day passed. Henry came back. It helped to do a few chores, and of course the cows and other animals had to be tended to. Listlessly we tried to begin cleaning up the mess of broken glass and other things in the kitchen.

We fixed some supper and ate in silence.

"Y'all want me an' Jeremiah ter stay da night in da barn, Miz Kathleen?" Henry asked.

"If you don't mind, Henry," replied Katie. "At least one of you. I just . . . we wouldn't want to be alone if . . . you know, if—"

"We's boff stay," said Henry. "Mr. Guiness an' Mr. Watson, dere biz'ness'll keep, ain't dat right, son?"

Jeremiah nodded.

"We be here jes' as long as you wants, Miz Kathleen," he said.

It got dark. It was a relief to go to bed. Mercifully I managed to sleep.

It wasn't till the next day that I even thought about the gold again. I came upon Katie out in the yard on her hands and knees trying to pick up what she could from the dirt.

"There was only a little of it left in the bag, Mayme," she said. "It's all mixed in with the dirt and gravel. All I can get is the bigger pieces."

Right then the thought of gold made me sick. How could something so lifeless be so powerful as to cause death? Who cared about the gold? Who cared about the bank and the loan and Rosewood?

What did it matter if they took it all away! Katie and I would have traded the whole plantation and the bag of gold and everything else just to have our father and uncle back.

He had been right—it wasn't worth anyone's getting killed over. His words from yesterday kept coming back to me over and over, and made me start crying every time I thought of them.

"*It's not worth anyone's getting killed over. We can take care of it. We're a family now . . . we don't need gold . . . all we need is each other.*"

The day brought no change. The doctor came as promised, changed Templeton's dressing, and left again, his face grim. He offered no words of hope, saying only "time will tell," and instructed us to talk to him and wipe his face with a damp cloth in hopes that it might help revive him.

We did as the doctor said, but every minute Katie and I were desperately hoping he'd wake up, even just for a moment, so that we could tell him we loved him. There's nothing else that seems to matter when a person is dying than that they know you love them.

Slowly the afternoon passed and another evening came.

By the following morning, the fearsomeness of his white form in the parlor wasn't so great as at first. We were accustomed to it now and that made it less frightening. Katie and I just wanted to be near him.

Like the doctor had suggested, we began sitting beside him, sometimes together as we quietly talked, sometimes alone. By that afternoon we were taking turns so that one of us would be with him every minute. Sometimes we just sat, sometimes we spoke softly or sang to him, sometimes we held his limp hand . . . sometimes we prayed.

But the longer it went on, the harder the waiting became, and the less likely it seemed that we would ever have the chance to say to him again what our hearts ached to say.

Crying Out to God

45

On the morning of the third day, I dozed off in the chair. I had been sitting with him most of the night. Katie came in and the sound of her steps awakened me.

"You need some sleep," she said. "I'll sit with him awhile."

But I didn't feel like sleeping. I went out for a walk.

Instead of walking toward the woods, I found myself heading along the border of one of the newly planted fields. I walked all the way around the length of the field, and before long was standing at the river. I sat down on the bank overlooking it and watched the water silently moving by. It looked so different now than a few months earlier when it had stretched from here nearly all the way to Rosewood, and just as far on the other side.

The words of Henry's prayer I had overheard as he knelt over Bilsby's body came back to me.

"I pray you won' be so muleheaded as you wuz on dis side ob dat ole ribber. . . ."

Was death like crossing a river, I wondered—a river like this? What was it like to die? What was my father going through right now? Was he aware in some corner of his being of standing on one side of a river and getting ready to step into the water, never to come out in this life again?

And what would it be like to come out on the other side? Would Jesus be waiting for him?

Slowly tears filled my eyes.

"Oh, God," I said softly as I began to weep, "I don't want him to die. I'm sorry if I'm not trusting you to do what's best . . . but I can't help it . . . I'm not ready to say good-bye to him forever!"

I was glad I was alone. It felt good just to cry as loud as I needed to without worrying that anybody could hear me.

So many things filled my mind. Strange as it is to say it since our time together had been so brief, mostly they were thoughts of the man I had always thought of as Mr. Daniels since the first day I laid eyes on him in his ruffled white shirt and moustache and winning smile, and only recently had finally been able to call *Papa*.

I thought about what he'd said.

"I had a few more things that I wanted to say to you."

As weak as he'd been, he had said what he needed to say, and was now at peace with me. I hoped he was also at peace with my mama, with himself, and with God.

But I had things to say too . . . things I *hadn't* said yet . . . hadn't said when I had the opportunity.

And now I was afraid it might be too late.

"Please, God . . ." I said, "please give me another

chance. I'm so sorry for the things I said that hurt him before, and for my wrong attitudes. Forgive my anger and selfishness. Please give me a chance to apologize to him, to really say I'm sorry so he knows I mean it, so he knows what a fine man I think he is. Please, God, give me another chance . . . don't let him die . . . I don't want to lose him now!"

Again I began to cry.

For so many years, tears had not come easily to me. I was practical, even stoic. I'd thought of Katie as the tender and emotional one, me as the practical one.

Now it seemed all I could do was cry! What had become of me? What was going on inside me! Who was this person I'd always thought I knew who now seemed so different, so full of feelings I didn't understand!

Was this what it was like to stop being a girl and gradually become a woman? Was growing up more than watching your body change, but watching your heart and feelings and thoughts change too?

Was this what happened when a girl discovered God . . . when she discovered love . . . when she discovered her father . . . when she discovered that she was feeling strange new things toward people and herself and life and the future?

It was so confusing! I had never felt such things before. Now a thousand emotions were tumbling about inside me all at once!

Gradually my thoughts stilled and my heart quieted.

Maybe it was fearsome and confusing to grow up, I thought. But there was a part of it that was a little exciting too. Right then the grief and guilt and fear in my heart were so strong I couldn't feel much of anything else. Yet I knew I didn't want to go back either. I didn't want to be the little slave girl again. If pain and grief were part of growing up, maybe I had to learn to face them, and learn from them . . . and be strong because of them.

I sat for a long time staring into the river, not so much thinking anymore how the river was like *death* but how it was like *life*—how it kept rolling along and how life kept bringing one new thing after another.

I don't know how long I'd been sitting there when I heard a sound behind me.

I turned. It was Jeremiah coming across the field. I stood up and smiled. He walked up the bank.

"How'd you know where to find me?" I said.

"I watched you go w'en you lef'."

Without any more words he took me in his arms. We stood for a minute or two, just stood there quietly. I felt at peace, almost like his embrace was an answer to the turmoil I had been feeling a short time earlier. I don't know why, but I sensed he understood something of what was going on inside me without my needing to say it. It was more than just our both being black. It was deeper than that.

We sat down together. Jeremiah took my hand and we sat, just staring into the river, neither of us saying a word. With death pressing upon us so close, it was a solemn time.

Twenty or thirty minutes later, gradually another sound intruded into my ears. I was so content, and starting to get drowsy again, that at first I didn't recognize it as meant for me.

I kept staring at the water below us, but as the sound gradually got louder and louder, slowly Jeremiah turned his head and glanced back over the fields.

Someone was running toward us.

"Mayme . . . Mayme!"

Now I heard it too. I turned and looked back toward the house in the distance.

It was Katie!

"Mayme!" she cried, now taking a shortcut from the way I had come and running straight across the field of dirt.

My heart seized with dread. I feared it had finally happened.

Jeremiah and I stood and hurried down the embankment.

"Mayme!" Katie cried again as she got nearer. "Come . . . hurry. He's awake!"

I left Jeremiah's side and ran toward her. I slowed when Katie and I met, but only long enough to make sure that I had heard her right. The look of joy on her face was all the answer I needed!

I dashed off toward the house, leaving Katie out of breath and hurrying to catch up with me.

A New Beginning
46

I flew into the house and ran straight for the parlor.

There he was with his eyes open. A little color had returned to his cheeks.

Emma and Aleta were standing on the other side of the room, a little timid to get too close. They still weren't quite sure whether he was going to die or not.

"Where've you been, little girl?" he said as I knelt down beside him, a huge smile on my face. "I've been asking everyone where you were."

His voice was soft and weak, but I detected the hint of a smile on his lips.

"Oh, Papa!"

"What's all this—I thought the tears were all done!"

"Almost!" I laughed—laughing and crying at the same time. "I'm sorry. I was just so afraid. I thought—"

"That I was going to die? Naw . . . I'm not going to

die! I told you that you and I were going to have a long talk, and that I was going to take you to Charlotte. And from now on, I intend to be a man who keeps his promises. I told you, I'm not about to lose you now."

I couldn't help laughing again through my tears. I was so happy!

"But I am about as thirsty as I've ever been in my life," he said. "How does a man get a drink around here?"

I jumped up and ran into the kitchen and pumped a glass of water. I ran back so fast I think I spilled half of it on the floor.

"And help me sit up," he groaned. "I'm sick of lying here."

I put one arm around his shoulders and tried to ease him up as he struggled forward. But he winced in pain from the effort.

"Aagh . . . ow—it hurts! What happened to me, anyway?"

"You got shot, Papa," I said. "You got shot saving Katie's life."

"Did I, now? Well, that sounds mighty heroic! Seems I do remember something about chasing her out of the house when suddenly everything went black."

"Can you sit up a little more and I'll give you a drink of water."

With my arm still around him, he managed to lean forward enough for me to get the glass to his lips.

"Ah, Mary Ann . . . that feels good," he said as he sipped at it. I tipped the glass higher until he managed to drink down the whole thing. "I need more. I'm parched!"

Within minutes all of us were clustered around, all

talking at once and trying to help him get comfortable and dashing upstairs for pillows and blankets and running into the kitchen for water and asking what he wanted to eat and scurrying and bustling about in a beehive of chatter and activity.

How suddenly life had returned to Rosewood!

"My, oh my," he said, laughing lightly, "I don't know if all this attention is good for me!"

"It be good fer us, Mr. Daniels!" said Emma. "We all thought you wuz gwine ter die, an' it's been so quiet roun' here I jes' about cudn't stan' dat silence no mo!"

Emma's words filled the whole room with laughter!

That evening, after we had gotten him into a new clean shirt of Katie's daddy's, he tried to stand up. But he was too weak and lightheaded to last more than a few seconds. But when he started to eat he quickly began to gain his strength back.

In another few days he was on his feet on and off throughout the day, though still weak and had to stay in bed a good part of the time. By then he was eating like a horse and drinking gallons of water and coffee and was joking and laughing just like his old self. Dr. Jenkins came back out, changed the dressing and bandage again, and pronounced himself amazed at the rapid recovery, though every time he came we had to go into our pretending again about Katie's mama still being around.

Katie, now the practical one and acting more and more like the mistress of a plantation every day, was the first to bring up the loan again.

"Uncle Templeton," she said one day, "Mama's loan is due next week. What are we going to do?"

"I'll go and see that banker of yours," he said. "I'll tell him everything."

Katie looked away and he saw the look of hesitation on her face.

"What is it?"

"I . . . I'm just not sure I want everyone in town to know yet," she said. "I'm still a little nervous about what might happen."

Her uncle thought a minute.

"I understand," he said. "By the way, whatever happened to the gold?"

"It was still just lying out on the ground," answered Katie. "I picked up most of it, though there's some dirt mixed in with it."

"Three hundred dollars' worth?"

"I don't know—I think so. Do you want to see?"

"Let's have a look."

Katie brought the bag from where she had been keeping it in one of the drawers of the parlor sideboard. Her uncle took it, felt it in his hand, and looked inside.

"Three hundred dollars easy," he said. "Probably five or six. Tell you what . . . I've got a few connections in Charlotte. Let's hitch up your best wagon. I propose that we all go into Charlotte—all five of us—"

"Dere be six ob us, Mr. Daniels," said Emma. "Don't fergit my William!"

"Six of us indeed!" he laughed. "I propose, then, that the *six* of us go into Charlotte. We shall sell the gold there for cash to take care of your mama's obligation with the bank. And if I might be permitted to borrow twenty or thirty dollars from the proceeds, Kathleen, which I will pay back along with what I owe your mama's cigar box," he added with a wink, "I would like to buy my four young ladies all brand-new dresses!"

The room erupted in celebrations and shouts of anticipation.

"But can you, Papa," I said, "can you ride that far?"

"You keep pouring food into me for another few days and I'll be fit for anything!"

"And *you* need a new ruffled shirt, Uncle Templeton," said Katie. "The one you were wearing got too much blood on it. I threw it away."

"A new shirt it is!"

He paused and a strange look came over his face.

"But . . ." he added after a moment, "no more ruffled shirts for Templeton Daniels."

"Why not, Uncle Templeton? I would hardly recognize you in anything else."

He laughed with delight.

"The fact is, Kathleen," he said, growing serious again, "I want to put the past behind me, poker and ruffled shirts and running from my responsibilities. I want to make a new beginning . . . it will be a new beginning for all of us."

"Then what kind of shirt will you wear?" I laughed. I couldn't imagine him in anything but fancy clothes either.

"A good sturdy work shirt, Mary Ann," he said. "If I'm going to become a Shenandoah County farmer and cotton grower, I have to look like one. And just maybe we'll get a pair of work trousers and boots to go with the work shirt.—What do you think, Kathleen?" he added, glancing toward Katie. "May I borrow enough for that too?"

"There wouldn't be anything if it weren't for you,

Uncle Templeton. You saved Rosewood. It's yours just as much as it is mine. It's all of ours *together*."

"Thank you, Kathleen. And our being together . . . that's all we need, if you ask me."

We were all so excited about the trip to Charlotte we began making plans immediately. None of us could talk about anything else. Papa even said he knew of a hotel where he had stayed a few times that allowed colored folks inside that he would take us to, and where we would eat dinner in a fancy restaurant and even spend the night. I couldn't imagine that anything could sound more exciting!

And it was too. We had the time of our lives!

The morning after we returned from Charlotte six days later, Katie was up early preparing to go to town. She'd convinced Papa that his going would only raise more unwanted questions than if she went herself. But we did ask Jeremiah to come out and ride in with her. She didn't want to go all that way to the bank alone carrying over three hundred dollars in cash money.

As soon as the buggy was out of sight, Papa left the yard where we had been standing watching them go. He walked out past the barn, then toward the field where we had planted the cotton. He walked slowly, like he was looking at everything for the first time. He looked so different in his new work clothes.

I watched him as he stooped down in the middle of the dirt to examine the tiny little shoots of green that were just starting to pop through the soil.

It was wonderful to see. It was indeed like watching a new beginning, just like he'd said—a new beginning inside a person.

After about a minute I walked after him. He heard me coming, stopped and waited, then stretched out his arm and pulled me to his side as we continued on.

"Well, Mary Ann," he said, "I think it's time you show me around this place so that as soon as Kathleen gets back we can decide what's to be done."

Katie did get back several hours later, laughing and happy and with stories to tell about Mr. Taylor's surprise when she'd plopped that three hundred and fifty dollars down on his desk—in cash this time!—and all the questions he'd asked. By then Papa and I had walked around Rosewood, as much as he could, and I'd had the chance to say a lot of the things I wanted to say to him. I was happy too, though in a different way than Katie.

We both had been given back something we'd thought we'd lost.

She had her plantation. But I had been given back something even better.

I had my father.

EPILOGUE

A HORSEMAN ENTERED GREENS CROSSING, North Carolina, early in the year 1867 carrying legal documents that he hoped would establish his claim to one of the large nearby plantations.

The meeting several months before at a Charlotte garden party had been as accidental as it had been, in the rider's view, fortuitous.

Marvin Taylor had been but a passing acquaintance when he was just getting started in the financial business years before. That had been long before the war. From a prominent Charlotte family, he and Taylor were of similar age and their paths had crossed on several occasions. He had not thought of Taylor in years and had had no idea that he was now managing the bank of the small town near where his brother lived some twenty miles northeast of the city.

Then they chanced to meet at the garden party, had shared a mint julep or two followed by a glass of bourbon. Gradually the talk between them had turned in the direction of their mutual acquaintance. That's when the conversation had become interesting.

The man's name was Burchard Clairborne. His first stop would be at the bank.

Watch for volume four
of SHENANDOAH SISTERS

Together Is All We Need

To share your thoughts with the author,
to receive a complete listing of his books,
or to subscribe to
LEBEN,
a periodical dedicated to the spiritual vision of
Michael Phillips and the legacy of George MacDonald
($20/year, issued quarterly), please contact:

Michael Phillips
LEBENSHAUS INSTITUTE
P.O. Box 7003
Eureka, CA 95502